Perfect Flower

Elizabeth Howliston

First published in Great Britain as a softback original in 2019

Copyright © Elizabeth Howliston

Edited by Martin Rickerd

The moral right of this author has been asserted.

Typeset in Baskerville

Design, typesetting and publishing by UK Book Publishing

www.ukbookpublishing.com

ISBN: 978-1-912183-96-8

Book One

Prologue

To John

I cannot promise perfect recall after all these years, but you asked me if I would write something of the family history. I hope you will see that I have done a little more than that. I have welcomed the opportunity, because my aunt and uncle were very extraordinary people. As a child I was fascinated by objects which lay in odd corners in the old house: the ivory counters, an elephant footstool and dusty drawings of orchids. I can close my eyes and remember the smell of dust and patchouli. These old things seemed to occupy their own special place, and even the dry-stone pond and its broken fountain had charm. The old house seemed perfect to me. To this day it occupies a precious place in my heart.

I have remembered the most curious things in undertaking this work – stories of life in India, the wealth gained and lost in pursuit of that perfect flower, the opium poppy. The East India Company's activities in India are shocking to modern ideas, but how marvellous to have among our ancestors such pioneering spirits. To assist in my research I have the paintings which you have always admired, and an old sketchbook with watercolour drawings and pencil sketches, which have helped me to remember. I am very grateful that the rest of the family has trusted me with their own precious letters and memories. I think that some of my correspondents have divulged more than they intended, as there has been a degree of secrecy over the years.

When I was young I listened to their stories. I learned that time means nothing under the spotlight of a good memory. The years dropped away from them as they spoke. I will always remember their vivacity, the constancy and balance of it all. It was such a place of safety for me. The silence regarding my own parents is harder to explain. I have long since forgiven them; what else can I do? I have to tell you that writing this book has been unexpectedly unsettling; the circumstances surrounding my own birth were not known to me. I was surrounded by the most loving family – how could I have suspected? I was always told my parents were abroad, but I suppose there are skeletons rattling away in every family closet. I remember being told that my father had died. They told me in such a casual way, as if to say, 'It doesn't matter to you now, darling, it happened years ago, we just thought you were old enough now to know these things'. I also knew that my mother had remarried; it must have been mentioned in my company. They were not cruel people – they just dropped things into conversation when we were all quiet together. I feel now that it must have been to avoid awkward questions and any embarrassment. My real life was with them; I really thought nothing about it. I certainly felt no sense of loss. I had never known either parent; they were never part of my life so I never questioned any further, until now.

You will forgive me if I refer to those who were close to me by their Christian names. I always referred to John and Julia in this way and I want you to better understand them. John and Julia Deuchars were cousins on my mother's side, and they brought me up with care and kindness when they had no reason to do so. I truly loved them. I remember they got me a dog and we called it 'Darling'. Unless I asked awkward questions, they called me 'Darling' too. If I touched a nerve, as children sometimes do, I would get that look I have sometimes given to you. They could be difficult, perfectly oyster-like, when they chose. I will not take anything away from their memory, my beloveds. I feel you should know it all now.

I hope, also, that you will forgive a little embellishment; I have always wanted to write a book. With so much material close to home, it has been no great effort. My darling John Robert, this is for you. Please accept the story of our family and my birth with all my love.

Your Gramps.

Contents

Prologue I

Chapter One 1

Chapter Two 25

Chapter Three 39

Chapter Four 51

Chapter Five 61

Chapter Six 71

Chapter Seven 75

Chapter Eight 87

Chapter Nine 111

Chapter Ten 129

Chapter Eleven 141

Chapter Twelve 163

Chapter Thirteen 179

Epilogue 185

Glossary 187

Chapter One

There is much to be said for an uneventful childhood – no financial storms to wreck family fortunes, no removal to a grimy mill town or suggestion of forced emigration. Parents who are encouraging create children with confidence and a cheerful disposition. These children grow up under a cloudless sky. My first cousin once removed and guardian, John Deuchars, was fortunate in having such a childhood. Looking back, it might have been helpful had he experienced a little adversity in preparation for adult life. He was perhaps a little spoiled. John was enrolled in school later than was usual, but he was liked and did well both academically and on the field. Sporting prowess always guarantees a respectable number of friends.

John was sent to study at East India College at Hailey in Hertfordshire aged sixteen. It was intended that he train as a writer and he was fortunate enough to be enrolled there during the time of Thomas Malthus. John learned Latin, Greek, Accounting, Law, Morality and some rudiments of native languages. He showed considerable artistic promise; his drawing even attracted the attentions of the cartographer. Responding well to discipline and hard work, everyone at Hailey felt that he would do very well indeed.

I have wondered if John should have encountered some check in his younger years. He could have fought over the rope swing near the river, bloodying his nose to protect what was his. It might have been better for him because he would have learned to fight. It would have taught him that there are times when it is important to make a stand. John was taught that high standards and hard work were all that was required. He was not made aware that there are people who scheme, cheat, and fight like tigers. He did not know that a less careful upbringing produces strength of a different kind.

John Deuchars at eighteen was tall, and graceful in his movements. Always thoughtful and easy in his manner, he was confident in himself and secure in the devotion of family and close friends. He was enthusiastic in those days, optimistic about his future, but acutely aware that his options did not include university or the Grand Tour. His family in the Parsonage at Deerfield were not the centre of what passed as local society; however, their company was sought by people who valued good council. John's father, the Rev. Edward Deuchars, carefully managed many difficulties brought to his door. Visitors were always made comfortable in his neat little study on the south-east side of the Parsonage. Edward Deuchars provided the best advice he could, although some of his opinions might have surprised his Bishop.

The Parsonage was unremarkable, a red-brick house unwisely facing the worst of the winter weather and set in unremarkable grounds. It had no impressive topiary but its greenhouses were productive. It was famous for its ancient row of beech trees, much too large for the narrow drive. In front of the house sat a stone pond. From the front bedrooms on a fine morning there was even a glint of the sea. The house had good chimneys and a welcoming entrance hall leading to spacious living rooms in the front, and kitchens and pantries at the back. These pantries were filled by regular deliveries from Deerfield Hall, courtesy of Colonel Roberts, younger step-brother to Edward Deuchars. They emptied all too quickly to meet the needs of the local community.

The close bond between the Deuchars brothers was forged when Edward was cut out of a will. Refusing to marry where his family chose, he earned their displeasure. The living at Deerfield, which included the Parsonage, was given to him by Colonel Roberts, and this rescued him and his young family. The same exacting Deuchars later took issue with Colonel Roberts' own choices. Family disapproval did not alter the Colonel's situation – he could afford to ignore them all. In addition to the Deerfield estate, the Colonel had inherited substantial property from his mother's family in the East Indies. The Roberts Shipbuilding Company was famous, and in his mother's family name he inherited the whole enterprise.

The Deuchars family may have been unforgiving but the Colonel never forgot the support and the welcome provided to his own bride by Edward Deuchars and his wife, Eleanor. In the eyes of the Deuchars both men had failed in their duties and responsibilities, and Deuchars' monies and properties were settled elsewhere. It is unfortunate that Edward Deuchars' disinheritance left him a relatively poor clergyman. John Deuchars, his son, would have to earn his own living.

There were mixed feelings about John going out into the world. It had always been understood that there were insufficient funds to support him as a gentleman. Fortunately, Colonel Roberts secured a place at Hailey through his connections with the British East India Company; everyone agreed it was extremely good of the Colonel to arrange things so nicely. The Colonel, anticipating John's graduation, made sure of a position for him in the East India Company's London offices in Leadenhall Street. There was an ever-increasing appetite for teas, tobacco and spices – who better to bring these delightful things home than John?

Colonel Roberts, with contacts in the India Board, arranged matters in the usual way. He asked that his nephew receive a preferential consideration prior to departure. This created a small income for the family at the Parsonage. John would take up a position on 4th January 1829, under the guidance of Mr Hugh Mowbray, previously of Messrs Jennings and Pewter. Mr Mowbray was well known and would take John under his wing. It was agreed that John would live with the Mowbrays, within walking distance of the Company's offices. In the fullness of time he would accompany Mowbray to India.

John knew he was fortunate to have this opportunity. Some of his tutors had spoken of their experience at first hand or of family service with the East India Company. They described the riches of the maharajas' palaces, the choking dust of the plains, vast rivers, and the rich ochre of the countryside. John could almost smell the scented air. What should concern him? – he was young and ambitious. He would learn his trade in London and then, after an appropriate period, he would secure an appointment and go to India. He was keen to begin, but first he would spend Christmas with his family.

Deerfield Hall was impressive; its accommodation outshone anything offered in the Parsonage. The rooms at the Hall were spacious, offering every convenience – but it was not a place of ease. Family gatherings were always in the cramped Parsonage, with its shortages of coal and hot water, and overworked kitchen. One recent arrival had already made herself comfortable in the blue guest room. Eleanor's cousin Sylvia deposited her daughter, Helen – my own mother – in the Parsonage for Christmas. Always resourceful, it took my mother no time to rectify her own situation by raiding the adjoining rooms. She had made herself known in the kitchen to ensure that she had a good supply of hot water, bread to toast, and a full coal scuttle.

I am told that Sylvia's habit of dropping off my mother at the Parsonage gates was famous. Eleanor frequently berated Sylvia, but she always helped when she could and this frequently included caring for Helen. Sylvia called in en route for London, still in search of her husband, Daniel Jennings, who had left his small family in Durham four years previously. He had left with his regiment, but never arrived with them in London and had not been heard of since. However, Sylvia had not given up hope. He had not been a good husband when his whereabouts had been known, and was a worse one by virtue of his absence. Despite all his faults, though, Sylvia would not hear a wrong word said against him.

After a silence of over four years, repeated enquiries from his wife, and a degree of embarrassment, the regiment had let it be known that he was not, to their knowledge, deceased. It emerged that he had been bought out at the time of his disappearance. There was a suggestion that there had been some unpleasantness, but the commanding officer would not be specific. Sylvia, unable to appreciate that such a thing should not be discussed publicly, told everyone who would listen that her husband's enemies must have forced him to resign his commission. There was a great deal of bad feeling wherever his name was mentioned.

Sylvia continued to search for him and wrote frequently to Daniel's fellow officers, but received nothing new in the excruciatingly polite replies. Eventually, his former chief begged her not to contact the regiment again. Daniel Jennings appeared to have vanished. It also became known that Colonel Roberts had known that Jennings had been bought out but decided to say nothing. The Colonel, defending himself, said that he was acting in the interests of the family. He arranged for a small income to be sent to Sylvia via the regiment. Unaware of his kindness and determined to find fault with everyone except her missing husband, Sylvia called the Colonel deceitful to his face. She vowed never to speak to him again. In this, Sylvia, my grandmother, maintained her lifelong habit of finding fault in persons most worthy of credit, and failing to lay blame where it was due.

There had been a vague rumour in the autumn of 1828 that Jennings had made contact with an army friend in London. Sylvia, against all advice, set out in a last attempt to find her 'dear Jennings'. She did this partly out of desperation, borrowing monies for travel from – of all people – her landlord. Sylvia felt that family hospitality and generosity were already exhausted, and creditors were pressing her daily for money. It was becoming impossible to manage without a husband, even a mediocre one. She was also pursued by people to whom Daniel Jennings owed money, and some of the demands had become frightening. The family at Deerfield were unaware of the deteriorating position. Sylvia was not yet desperate enough to tell them, but she spared her daughter Helen none of the details. Eleanor was a kind woman who said that allowances must be made for the behaviour of both mother and daughter. It was acknowledged that my mother's home life had been unconventional and that this accounted for her manners and disconcerting maturity. A girl of average size and a little older than her cousins, she was outspoken and confident, direct to the point of rudeness.

Helen Jennings was passionate, pretty and determined. I have been told that, when she smiled, her face assumed a warmth and beauty which made men look at her, and she knew it. Her hair was thick and jet-black, she had a fine complexion, and her eyes were large and grey. Her dress was, out of necessity, plain, but her figure was not. She felt the difficulties of her current situation but was not discouraged. It was simply not in her nature to become despondent. Her glass was always 'half full'; she knew she would not always be poor.

Unused to regular hours, she found the early family breakfast a trial. Sunday was her least favourite day. One particularly frosty morning Helen argued that she had said everything to the Lord she wanted to say from her bedside, so there was no need for her to go out into the cold to repeat herself. This was not strictly true, as she had asked the Lord several times to arrange for her to have some money because she currently had none. Her gloves were mostly of darning material, so she included in her prayers a request for a new pair, but none had materialised.

On this occasion Eleanor insisted, 'Good things will bear a second saying'. So Helen was coaxed into getting out of bed and going to church. It made her bad tempered. After lunch she declared herself tired and stretched out on the sofa, which was unused to persons lying full length upon it. Eleanor instructed Helen to sit up.

Elizabeth Deuchars, Helen's cousin, was affectionate and thoughtful. It was with pride that Eleanor observed Elizabeth's many kindnesses to her. Eleanor's teaching regarding behaviour to others had taken a strong hold. At fifteen, Elizabeth was practical and loved music. She would have adored a pianoforte but had to be content with her aunt's old spinet. Although the best of instruments when purchased, it had become weary in its damp quarters at the Parsonage.

Edward junior was nine years old and virtually lived among the trees at the edge of the Parsonage's drive. It was he who announced the arrival of a carriage making careful progress along it. It was a carriage everyone except Helen recognised, but she slid off the sofa curious and pressed her black ringlets against the windowpane. She edged Elizabeth aside just as the carriage drew up at the door and her cousin announced, 'Helen, it's Aunt Marianne. Now at last the holiday has really begun. We are so very near Christmas. Are you excited?'

Helen looked unmoved, answering, 'Does she have lovely clothes?'

'Oh yes, beautiful clothes – wait until you see her. But it is her manner which is lovely. Aunt Marianne can speak fluent French and she plays the pianoforte beautifully. We love her so much and she is delighted to be in young company. She says our vivacity reminds her of her own young life.'

Helen was not listening to nonsense about music or the old woman's girlhood. She had heard the maid talking of Madam Roberts, who had been taken to India with her first husband. Helen had questioned the maid about it. She listened carefully to the story of Marianne's return to England as a young widow. Helen imagined silk dresses with long purple trains, cerise ostrich feathers and bright scarves fastened around the heads of turbaned attendants. Furs, robes, servants – she would have them all. She intended to be mistress of a significant establishment when she grew up. She pictured herself as a grown woman covered in jewels. She would be surrounded by red-coated admirers and clouds of perfume. Her future would be bright, and as she closed her eyes she thought of the lovely things she meant to possess and the men she meant to captivate. There would be no more making do, absolutely no need for darning needles.

There is always change when a new influence exerts itself in a settled family. Observing how crowded the window was becoming, Eleanor turned to Helen.

'Please, dear, go to the door and meet Mrs Roberts. She is not strong, and you can give her your arm.'

Helen appeared not to hear, and Eleanor repeated the request.

'I would much rather not,' Helen replied. 'Elizabeth has said she wants to help Aunt Marianne. If she is as ill as you say, I think Elizabeth gentler and more suited to the task than I.' This was true.

Eleanor wondered where such self-confidence had been acquired and how a girl of almost sixteen years should be so infuriating. She recalled Helen's mother and, with more discomfort still, Helen's father. Determined to persist in her training of this wilful little woman, she said:

'I think you will find that in helping Aunt Marianne you will be close to her when she brings out her gifts. She always likes to give them to you all as soon as she arrives. I will add, however, that it is important to think of someone other than yourself, of what you might do to help others. Please do as I ask, dear, and get up from that couch and go and welcome your aunt.'

Helen looked smilingly at Eleanor and sighed as if humouring her.

'If I had not thought only of myself all these years past, Cousin Eleanor, nobody else would have done so. I am used to thinking in this way out of necessity and I cannot give it up.'

Eleanor had heard this sort of thing before. It should have been heart-rending, but it was said with such disrespectful lightness that it was difficult to avoid feeling very cross. She did not like the way the child behaved, but it was not her fault. Eleanor was sure that

Helen felt all the hurts of her young life. Helen stood with eyes fixed above Eleanor's head, feeling pleasure in regarding Eleanor's raised colour when referred to as 'cousin'. Sylvia had expressly said she must address Eleanor as 'Aunt' or 'Ma'am'. When challenged about her lateness for meals or her behaviour, the words 'Cousin Eleanor' seemed to just pop out of her mouth.

Sylvia revealed little about their circumstances; her letters to the Parsonage had been infrequent. Most of them asked if anything could be spared for Helen's tuition. Eleanor observed that the child neither played an instrument, danced, nor spoke any languages; Helen had none of the usual accomplishments of a young lady. The small amount of money she had been able to send must have been used to keep a roof over their heads and food in their mouths. She recalled Sylvia's determination to marry against her mother's advice so many years before; Eleanor had encouraged Sylvia to follow her heart, so shared some of the blame for what had come to pass.

Helen walked into the hall just as the carriage door was opened and the steps lowered. A tall man emerged, followed by a very small, graceful woman who carefully descended, looking around her as if surprised by everything she saw. Pale and very thin, with wisps of grey hair curled at the temples, small lines were etched around once lovely lips. Marianne was unwell again, and it was clear that every effort made her tired. Helen stepped forward and, in spite of herself, offered her arm. Their hands met, and Helen felt the frail grip of Marianne's tapering fingers through soft blue leather gloves. Those fingers would crush so easily – it was just as if a tiger had a lamb in its paws.

'You have grown up while I was not looking,' said Marianne in the softest of voices.

'I would hope I had,' Helen replied quickly. 'When last you saw me I was only a child.'

Turning carefully, Helen helped Marianne through the Parsonage door.

'I am to see you to your chair.'

Helen pushed Elizabeth back towards the stairs, out of her aunt's reach. She had decided to make a favourable impression for, although Elizabeth had the advantage of established intimacy, this could be changed. What had they said about Marianne liking to be amused? If she could encourage a partiality, who knew what might follow? Helen felt she could be very vivacious indeed if required, and hoped that this beautiful woman might understand her situation. She might even remove her difficulties or, at least, notice her lack of decent clothing. Her mother had said that Marianne was independently wealthy but had married for love that was proof of feeling.

According to the maid, when her young husband had died Marianne quickly remarried, to a wealthy man. Helen resolved to make Marianne and her rich husband help her – she was family and they had money. She would tell Marianne something of her difficulties.

As Marianne stopped and turned back towards the door, a graceful young man appeared at her side. Charles, her only son, was seventeen, just one year younger than John but quite small for his age. He had not been expected to survive his first year, but had a strong constitution and a stronger will. The family did not make comparisons between Charles and John. Charles's personality and wit always gave the impression of a larger-than-life figure. He was the family miracle and his mother's joy. He frightened Marianne with his determination to study medicine or to become a soldier. He reminded her so much of his father.

The Colonel privately thought a career as a soldier a first-rate idea for his stepson, but was always sparing with his opinions about the boy. He never suggested any course at variance with Marianne's views. Colonel Roberts did not risk discord between himself and his beautiful wife. The boy had come unlooked for and unexpected, growing into a perfect likeness of his father. It was the most natural thing in the world to care for his best friend's widow and her unborn child. But Charles had turned his mother's hair grey, and by mutual agreement there were no others. The Colonel was determined to hold on to his frail, beautiful wife for as long as he could. He sacrificed the chance of his own heir but it was not essential he produce a child. Charles and his brother Edward's children would suffice. He cared for Charles as if he were his own, a promise made to a long-dead friend. After all, he had Marianne for a whole lifetime.

Marianne knew that her beloved's face was forever preserved in this image of young manhood. It was therefore both a source of joy and pain to Marianne and Colonel Roberts to observe the increasing likeness of son to father. They had always spoken of Charles's father openly, as he had been dear to both. Charles possessed an excellent mind and an intensity which made him seem older than his years. He was comfortable in company, with a self-confidence unusual in the young. His uncle had commented more than once that Charles had a very fine brain and would do well in university. Edward Deuchars had taught him Latin and Greek, and he learned quickly.

The room was full of warmth and laughter, but Charles noticed that his cousins, Elizabeth and Victoria, were left outside the festivities. He looked over to where Helen stood close to his mother. She had John at her elbow and was insisting he untie the large basket full of gifts which she had set at Marianne's feet. Charles intervened.

'Have patience – stand back! We have just arrived. There is no great hurry for present giving, is there? In any event, we usually wait until everyone has had refreshment. Come, make room – my mother is too crowded.'

He moved a chair close to his mother and made Elizabeth sit. He firmly took Helen's arm and handed her his mother's gloves and a fine purple silk scarf. Charles signalled towards the door, where a maid was still waiting.

'Helen, I am so pleased to see you again. We are going to need to get to know each other better, I think. Could you please take my mother's gloves and scarf?'

Helen was astonished.

'How dare you instruct me to take these to a servant? Who are you to tell me what I must do?'

But Charles had turned away while she was holding the gloves and scarf, and nobody could hear her above the noisy conversation. She knew that she was going to do as Charles asked, which made her furious. Who on earth did he think he was?

Helen determinedly remained at Marianne's side in order to receive the gifts, which she intended to take from her and hand out. It was time for Elizabeth to receive her gift; Charles stayed close to his mother, waiting for Helen to receive her present.

'Mother, do you not think that, as Helen has her gift, Elizabeth could help you now?'

Without another word, he gathered up the remaining gifts and placed them in Elizabeth's lap. There was no malice; he had an authority of manner but did not intend to wound. Charles was just taking care of his cousin.

Helen withdrew from the family group and watched them from her new place beside the window. She had handed the gloves to the maid, but not the silken scarf, which she now wound tightly around her fingers. It was so soft and lovely to touch that she decided to keep it. She secreted the scarf inside the sleeve of her dress, sure that nobody had seen her. She watched Charles, his arm lovingly placed on his mother's shoulder.

Elizabeth handed out the remaining presents. Helen had been excluded, and picked at the frayed edge of her sleeve. The giving of presents may seem such a small thing and it should be pleasurable, but how often is this not the case? We remember giving a delightful gift, only to receive something which we do not value. Helen knew what she would have liked but her package had revealed a needlework case, which made her furious. Anyone could see that her clothes were beyond mending. Elizabeth had received a nice pair of gloves and there were other plump packages lying there for the taking. She had intended to cultivate Marianne, but that was not the only way to manage things.

Helen considered her circumstances and decided that some people had more than they needed. She wanted the things Marianne had – beautiful clothes, an adoring husband, the wealth to do as she pleased. Colonel Roberts moved from his chair and took Marianne by the hand. Most of the presents were now distributed, but some remaining parcels were placed on a side table. They sat invitingly among home-made sugared almonds and marzipan sweetmeats. Helen could hardly take her eyes off them.

Eleanor looked anxiously out of the window. The narrow driveway was in shadow. This was to be John's farewell before leaving for London to start his new career. He and his father were late. It was suggested that the ladies should change in readiness for dinner. The girls made their way upstairs, Helen last of all. It would not take her long to prepare, as she had only two dresses. As she still wore her hair long, swift brushing was all that her black curls needed. She walked slowly up the stairs, holding a parcel concealed in her skirts. Just as she was about to run to her room she heard the front door open, and two men came into the hall.

Helen watched from where no one could see her. It might have been the reflection of the candles in the mirror, but all light appeared to fall upon the younger man. He turned as a figure emerged from the living room. Helen saw Eleanor closing her eyes as she embraced her son. They held each other close for a long time. Helen shrank back into the dark stairwell. So much beauty, so much love – too much of everything in this house and what do I have?

Upstairs she watched as the wrappings burned in the hearth. Placing the scarf with a pair of blue kid gloves in the bottom of her trunk, she listened. Everything was quiet. She closed the trunk, pushed it back under the bed, and felt so much better.

The seating at dinner was not as Helen would have wished. The adults were enjoying a conversation with John at the head of the table. Helen could not hear what they were saying. She looked down at her faded summer dress and then at Elizabeth's and Victoria's matching red gowns. She was unable to speak to Aunt Marianne or to attract John's attention. Her cousins were talking about music; she knew about music but nobody asked her. Helen placed her elbow on the table and decided that she would make no contribution at all. She looked crossly at Colonel Roberts, who smiled and raised his glass to her. Helen was bored with these children. She decided that they had not placed her near Aunt Marianne on purpose.

A voice from the top of the table called out to her.

'Cousin Helen, I am so pleased you are with us. It is important to me that we are all together, especially this year.' John continued, 'Do you sing? I propose we get up after dinner, with my mother's permission, and have some music.'

'Yes, Cousin. I do sing. What would you prefer? I have a number of songs by memory. I have been told I have a very pretty voice and that I am very expressive. They said I could make my way on the stage.'

The room quietened a little.

'Who told you that?' demanded Eleanor. 'No tutor would say such a thing. I am sure in your mother's drawing room you would not have been spoken to in such a way.'

'No indeed, Ma'am,' said Helen, 'but there are all kinds of tutors.'

Helen afforded Eleanor her title; it was Christmas, after all. She thought ruefully of the rooms which served as her mother's living quarters. There was certainly no drawing room, but what would these people know about how they lived?

'It was the officers in my father's regiment who told me I was expressive. They tossed me shillings, which I should have liked to keep. The gentlemen said that I put so much into my voice and eyes. They said I had a natural talent. I often sang and danced for them.'

There was now a complete silence. Helen had not intended to give her aunt this description of life at home. It hadn't seemed so very shocking at the time, but she should have remembered that this family would think differently. They didn't have to please anybody and did not know what it was to live without comfort. John looked at Helen, then at his mother.

'I am sure, Cousin, that you are a most beautiful singer and an accomplished dancer.'

Charles was amused.

'We only have Cousin Helen's word that her voice is lovely. But, no matter, we will judge her abilities later. I will sing with her myself if she is any good, but I will not be tossing her money.'

Elizabeth smiled; everyone knew Charles could not sing.

The arrival of the pudding was timely, the smell of spices drifting across the table. Conversation quickly turned to John's new venture. Colonel Roberts asked him how long he was to remain at home.

'I am home for one week and two whole days, sir, then I leave for London.'

'What do you hope for, John?' his Aunt Marianne asked softly.

All eyes turned towards him.

'I hope to distinguish myself in my life and bring honour and credit to my family.'

'What?' said Helen, far too loudly. 'Surely you wish to enrich yourself, and bring home jewels and silks and spices by the hundredweight. Do you not wish to experience the blazing hot sun, the sights and smells of India? Think of the maharajas, veiled women and wild animals. I have heard there are elephant-headed gods and rubies the size of hen's eggs.'

'Well,' said John, 'I have heard marvellous things, too. I confess I would like this new venture to be profitable and exiting. I hope to make a name for myself. I want to be a Company man.'

'Do not forget to paint – you must bring back paintings of elephants!' exclaimed Charles. 'We will exhibit them in London. I will come out to see you. Please arrange for me to ride through the jungle on the biggest beast you have.'

Elizabeth took up the theme, gripping Helen's arm much too tightly.

'You will have ready for our arrival, Brother, baskets of Helen's rubies, bolts of silk and all the tea we can drink.'

This caused much amusement to everyone except Eleanor and Marianne. John hesitated, looking at Marianne's beautiful face, then at Helen. He began to realise a very small part of what this new life might entail and how great a change was almost upon him.

'I will bring you rubies if you want them. I will bring back something for all of you.' As he spoke he looked at each of his family. 'If that is what would make you all happy.'

Helen looked at him and knew then that she ought to go with him. It was not completely unheard of for women to travel.

Colonel Roberts, holding his tearful wife's hand, raised his glass. 'A toast: to John!'

The whole house seemed to tremble on its foundations as the family stood and raised their glasses and chorused, 'To John!'.

Later, when the house was quiet and they were alone in their room, Colonel Roberts watched his wife as she removed the pins from her hair.

'I wish — rather, I hope — Marianne, that I have been right in sponsoring so complete a removal of this young man from his family. I would never forgive myself if he is unsuited or unequal to the task. I do not fear for him — that is to say, for any transgression of his. It is certain that he will be subject to the will and designs of those more experienced and less principled. I hope that he can withstand them. There have been some rather disquieting debates in Parliament about the Company's dealings since I made this arrangement.'

'Darling,' said his wife, 'I know we have our own bittersweet memories of India, but you have done your best for him. He is young and he must go out into the world. What else is he to do? There is no money to keep him at home. They must all grow up, you know.'

Marianne said this last absently, having enjoyed the security of husband and home for some years. She quite forgot, as she spoke, that her own darling — the rider of elephants — might also leave one day.

'I must,' she continued languidly, 'try to find some things I no longer need which might fit Helen. The child is positively threadbare.

She does not appear to have brought a scrap of decent clothing with her. I despair of Sylvia – how could she let the child come away without anything suitable to wear?'

Helen was torn between wanting so much to be part of the light and life around her and resenting everything about her cousins. Angry as she was with her own situation, she was caught up in the life and excitement that surrounded John. She resented the cosy tranquillity, the intimacy and clumsy attempts at kindness towards her. She had immediately discarded the doll she had been given by the sisters. What on earth would she do with a doll at her age? She had been a woman long since. They were such babies.

There had been some consolation – she had been given a pair of very smart boots. Aunt Marianne had supplied other essentials and she ought to have been grateful. She disliked being obliged to thank anyone for hand-me-downs, however beautiful they might be. It was not in her nature to be in debt; who wanted to be beholden to another person if it could be avoided? Helen was envious of the sense of security and peace which surrounded the Parsonage. They knew nothing about real people or about her life. It was hard to contain her anger, but she knew it would not always be so difficult.

On Old Year's Night, John and Helen were in their favourite place, the conservatory.

'I understand how difficult things are for you,' said John. 'If you need help, you know I am your friend. I know nobody speaks about your home and your father. It is because they don't know what to say to you. I think you are such a fine young woman. I am proud of you, proud to be your cousin.'

John was thoughtful and kind. He included her in all the celebrations and treats. He singled her out, and deflected awkward questions from unknowing guests at the Parsonage. It was as if he could read her thoughts. She enjoyed allowing him to take care of her, although she did not require this. The attention towards her was wonderful. He clearly felt something – why otherwise would he have been so kind and attentive? She wondered what could be arranged in the short time before his departure, and whether John realised how useful she could be to him. Helen decided to persuade him to take her to London.

The morning of John's departure arrived and the family were up early. The house and its occupants were not as bright and cheerful as usual. In the summerhouse Helen sat with Otter, the terrier, on her knee. She was stroking his russet hair and gazing into his black eyes. He poked his cold, wet nose into her hand. Helen stoked his big, feathery paws – he was some comfort.

She had carefully considered what she would say, but did not feel as calm as she would have liked. She hoped that John would know where to find her. She knew he would look for her where they had sketched and talked. She was his strong-willed and opinionated friend. They had laughed and argued together, but she wanted more.

John made a scraping noise on the gravel with his feet so that she could hear him coming. He had his spare handkerchief at the ready, having come from his tearful sister.

Helen knew his footfall. She was nervous but did not feel at all tearful. She would tell him she wanted to go with him to India, that he was the man she wanted to make a life with. She would tell him that she had energy and courage. Her father's officer friends had said that anyone who went to India would become very rich. They would marry and live among maharajas. John looked at her shining eyes and offered his handkerchief, but she pushed it away.

'I don't need that,' she said. 'I wanted to say something important to you before it is too late. I need you to promise me that you will not leave home without me. You need someone to take care of you. I think without someone like me you will not be able to manage. You have no idea what people are really like! In London you will be within reach of family, of me. In India there are so many pitfalls for someone like you. I could help you. When you complete your training, we could go to India together. We will be old enough to do what we like. We will make money – everyone who goes to India makes a lot of money. Father's friends say that others die if they don't know how to manage properly.' She saw his astonished face, but continued. 'I mean that you might need someone who knows what the world is like, someone who could help you. I understand how things really are. Your family do not need to know I am with you until we are married.'

John looked at her, standing in front of him with her fists clenched and eyes so full of life. He saw a beautiful girl. He could also see that she was dangerous, and it frightened him. What on earth could she mean, they could go to India? It would be a scandal. To think that she could accompany him, suggesting that they should not tell his family! He took her hands in his before speaking.

'It is just like you to worry about me, but please have more faith than this. I will have Mr Mowbray to show me how to go on. You know I am to live with his family. I will not be completely alone. As to my going to India, I shall not be going for some time.' He reached out and picked a late blossom, the last survivor of a hot summer, and held it gently. 'I really cannot discuss marriage – you are still so young. I have no prospects yet. We must both be patient.'

Helen stroked one of the large, dark-green leaves, digging her nails into its flesh.

'I thought that, spending time together as we have, you might see that I would be able to help you. I thought that you would take me with you. I know you have to work hard, but you will progress. In two years' time I will be as near to eighteen as makes no difference – quite old enough for marriage. We could make a life together.'

John saw nothing of the sort. She was lovely and he had enjoyed her company. He had even thought, when her hair brushed against his face, that it might be nice to sweep her into his arms. But he had checked himself – it was all out of the question as they were cousins. Nevertheless, he had wanted to spend time with Helen – she was exciting, she had entered into his plans, enthralled about his dream of travelling to India. However, what she now suggested – running off to India behind his family's back – what on earth could she be thinking? She had told him how difficult her life had been, and he believed they had become friends. This felt like a betrayal of his faith in her. She was such a lost soul – she must be made to see how improper it would be.

John tried to be gentle, and put his arm across her shoulders before speaking.

'You are a lovely girl, Helen, but I cannot say I will take you with me. I have no money, I have not made my fortune and I must think of my family first. They are depending upon me to make something of myself. I am indebted to Colonel Roberts, who has arranged my future. How could you think I could deceive them all? This is not how things are done.'

He was trying to be kind, but he failed. Helen had been sure she could persuade him. She knew he had not taken her seriously, and turned away. John begged her not to be cross.

'I thought you felt something for me,' was her riposte. 'I thought you understood something of what I am. I have lived and managed my own affairs. I am already older than you in my ways and I thought you understood that. Now you say "wait", but I have thought about everything. You don't need your family. I could help you. We could have the world, but you do not have the imagination to see it.'

John had overheard his mother talk about poor Helen and her difficult circumstances. He did not think carefully about the consequences of what he said. Looking at her sad face, he could not help himself.

'I do admire you, Helen. I have loved the time we have spent together. It is just that I have not begun my life yet. We must be patient and make what progress we can. I want so much to be successful and you have to believe that, with determination, we will each succeed in our own way. I know how difficult things are for you at home. Even if we are not together I will be thinking about you. We are good friends and, if I am able, I will always help you. You are a wonderful girl but how can either of us say what the future holds? I will be in London for a long time before I can get to India. We shall see each other at Deerfield. You must see that it is sensible to wait until we are older before deciding on something as serious as this.'

John hoped he sounded as if he had listened to her and would not hurt her feelings too much. He knew how gentle he needed to be with his cousin. He was disappointed that what he had seen as friendship had been misinterpreted. A mother's guidance was clearly absent in her case. Helen completely misunderstood him. She heard him say that they had time, that she was a wonderful girl. He had looked into her eyes and said they would see each other again. He would work hard in London and she would make her mother bring her to Deerfield when he came home for holidays. She would make him see that she was the kind of woman to help a man build a career. If he was not quite sure now, she would make him love her in time.

Helen reached into her sleeve.

'I am disappointed and may not forgive you, but you cannot refuse a keepsake. I have written a poem for you.' She unfolded the paper. 'I'm not sure why it came out like this but I wrote it while thinking of you. Remember that if you will go to London alone, I absolutely forbid you to leave for India without me. This poem describes what it would feel like if you did. I hope it makes sense to you. I never have any idea how these things will end once I begin them.'

She handed him the sheet of carefully written lines. John thought her strange, and wished he understood her. She was such a fascinating, unconventional girl, wholly without moral compass.

'Must I tell you again,' he replied with mock severity, 'that I am only going as far as London. I promise that I will keep your poem, always. If I do go to India some years from now and you are by some chance not with me, I will read it when I am sitting by the Hooghly.'

Helen knew he was treating her like a child. She made a grab for the sheet of paper but he was too quick. Pushing it into his waistcoat, he smiled.

'No, please Helen – it was lovely of you to write this for me. I will miss you, I will miss it all.'

John looked around the large greenhouse, with its lush plants sent over from Deerfield Hall, and took a deep breath. It made him dizzy, but orchids will do that. Helen sighed as John continued.

'If I could, I would pack my bags and go to London and then to India. If only I had money I could do exactly as I liked. I could make as much money in the East India Company as any man,' John said, looking down at her. 'We none of us here have very much money, Helen. I would not be leaving if it were possible. We must all make the best of our lives. The Colonel has been so kind and I have to go. You know that the Company does not allow young women in its employ.'

Helen felt his dismissal. John did not want them to argue now. He saw the tears welling up in her wonderful eyes. He nipped a flower with his fingers, trapping a bee so that it buzzed loudly in an effort to escape.

'I imagine you might be useful when I go out to look for specimens. You might wash my paintbrushes in fast-flowing rivers, being careful to avoid crocodiles. Heaven knows if I will have time to paint.'

He was talking about himself and the family not having money. It was ridiculous; she could not bear it. The bee was now furious, but John did not want to let it go in case it stung him.

'Please, Helen, do not be cross. Read your poem to me.' Then, more quietly, 'Please read it yourself, so that I might know how it should sound.'

She turned and looked directly at him. What good would a poem do?

'A decent poem reads itself, but in any case I see no point. Please let that bee go – it is wrong to hold him there.'

John did not understand her – it was only a bee. He looked down at the words she had written.

Flattening out the crumpled paper, he read:

Look out into the streaming sun, that shining ribbon of sea,
Think of us on a bright clear day when you are far from me.
See how I sparkle on top of the waves, part of the thundering roar,
Remember my love as the dawn comes up on a distant Indian shore.

'There is more, but it is unfinished,' said Helen.

John looked up as a tear ran down Helen's face, but she dashed his hand away. John was not offended. For some reason which he could not quite fathom, he pulled Helen's face towards his and kissed her slowly and gently on the lips.

Chapter Two

L ondon was quiet, most of society reluctant to stir after the
Christmas holiday, but business was briskly carried on where it
mattered. Holidays of more than one day were the province of
the wealthy, not the wealth earners.

'The wheels of industry grind continuously on and it is a good
thing for us that they do,' the gentleman said, panting as he walked.
'I could have done with you here before now, sir.' His breath caught
in his throat each time he spoke, and he spoke much. 'I suppose it
was hard to tear yourself away from dear friends. We were expecting
you three days ago, and the delay has been rather inconvenient. Your
family must dine often and well in the Christmas season among the
society of your district. I imagine you go back and forth?'

Hugh Mowbray strode arm in arm with his protégé towards
Craven House, the offices of the East India Company in Leadenhall
Street. The head of the Mowbray household was a small, balding
man, broad in the middle with short legs. Nobody could say he was
not well dressed; he took great care about his appearance. It was a
pity that locomotion was so difficult, for otherwise he would have
cut quite a figure. He was also prone to perspiring heavily, blaming
this on a fever contracted in Patna in 1825.

Hugh Mowbray thought he should have been Sir Hugh. This
was very unlikely to happen now. He had been unable to place
himself between a Governor-General and a *thagi*, contenting himself

instead with vicious commerce. He had not shone in complex negotiations or been the author of a spectacular trade coup. In his previous posting at Calcutta one or two of the Mahrattas had even got the better of him. He felt, nonetheless, that he was very well thought of where it mattered. Only recently he had been recognised in the street by one of the Board. He had once been mentioned in committee minutes, and he told John that things like that mattered. Mowbray was possessed of the most fabulous silk waistcoats and was as fastidious about his dress as he would have been had he actually been a member of the Board.

It had been a pleasure to oblige a friend of Colonel Roberts in taking on this young man, but on first impressions he appeared to be disappointing. Mowbray hoped he would be biddable, as he had no time for truculence in the young. Governors-General came and went with alarming frequency and the politics of the Board could be very deep. It was difficult to judge which favour might eventually return a dividend, but it was essential to oblige anyone with a connection. Mowbray was happy to declare himself delighted with John. He told Mrs Mowbray and the Mowbray girls that it was an honour to have been considered a suitable person to take charge of the young man.

He was also happy to assist because it did not presently inconvenience him. Many young men had come his way and he had taken them under his wing. They had gone out to India with him, and sadly some had not returned home. Hugh Mowbray viewed this as natural wastage. He always expected to be killed himself, and was relieved when he was spared. He did not think for too long about the poor young fellows who were not up to the mark.

Mowbray and John Deuchars were en route to inspect the offices and storage facilities in Blackwall. It was a bright, cold morning. Mowbray was, in spite of his physical disadvantages, setting a good pace. He felt sure John must be impressed with the organisation and the facilities – who would not be? He knew it was essential for the young and inexperienced to understand the basic nature and organisation of the Company before explanation of more complex areas of trade. Mowbray stopped to consult his pocket watch and was musing on his own value to the Company when he realised that his charge had pulled a small sheet of paper out of his coat pocket. He could hardly believe it – the boy was sketching the low wharf and the boats at anchor. *Sketching*, by God – and in broad daylight! He blamed himself – he had not instructed his apprentice for fully five minutes. John must understand that sketching was simply not done during business hours. Sketching was for evenings and Sunday afternoons with the ladies. Mowbray lost no time in starting his training programme in earnest. He grasped John by the elbow and steered him in a determined manner towards a wide door set low in the stonework. He pushed John along a short passage and into a small office.

The office contained a large desk and floor-to-ceiling shelves full of books and papers, with some curious-looking crates on the very top shelf. The desk was covered in writing materials, a large metal teapot and back issues of *The Gentleman's Magazine*. Mowbray squeezed behind the desk and threw himself into an old upholstered chair. He waved John to a low stool next to the shelves. It was January but Mowbray mopped his brow. His fingers moved rapidly over his blue silk waistcoat and lovingly fondled the ivory buttons which held everything firmly in place.

'I have now familiarised you with the marvellous environs of Company House. You have placed your foot on the first rung of your life's adventure and you may now make me some tea!'

While John was busy, Mowbray expounded on the Company.

'You will know that the India Board, our august commissioners, meet regularly in London to receive detailed reports of Company progress. By the way, I will not hear of it called the "John Company" – it has no dignity. Always refer to it by its correct name. The Board have caused the downfall of many a Governor-General of Bengal, however high and mighty their Excellencies might perceive themselves to be. The Company is a firm master when matters do not run smoothly in trade. In running the East India Company one has to remain alive to opportunity at all times, cultivate an astute mind, and keep one's wits about one. The company values a loyal servant and conscientious attention to …' – he paused, brushing a fleck off his waistcoat – '… detail.'

Mowbray nodded towards John's notebook, so John picked it up and began to write.

'The whole enterprise,' said Mowbray, 'is extremely valuable and relationships are delicately balanced, you understand my meaning? Our business is maximisation of profit and the interests of our shareholders – nothing must interfere with this. We do not meddle too much with the locals. There was some nonsense a short while ago about the burning of widows. This has been custom and practice for years in India. Interfering persons take issue with it and what do we have? What we have is trouble, that's what. We Company men turn a blind eye; we have always have turned a blind eye to local customs. We do so because we respect them, do you see? If the native wants to burn his poor dead brother's wife, why, we must humour him. As long as it does not interfere with business. Are you quite clear on that point before I continue?'

John had heard of *suttee* and regarded it as an abomination. He found his mentor's opinion surprising. John had been carefully raised, and could not help himself from speaking.

'Can any right-thinking Christian condone something on the grounds that it has been done for centuries? It goes against the morality which holds all human life sacred. When women who need our special protection are in danger, surely we must act to keep them from harm. I have understood that many of these women are very young, that they do not go willingly to the funeral pyre.'

Mowbray's mouth opened to speak, but to his complete astonishment John continued.

'I believe we may not hold sacrosanct a tradition if it is wrong. Is it not also the case that members of our own government are challenging Company rights to retain a monopoly in trade because we fail to address issues such as this? My father feels that more attention needs to be given to the careful management of India rather than a focus on profits alone. This concern would surely include the welfare of the people.'

Mowbray placed his thumbs into the two neat little pockets in his bright-blue waistcoat, pursed his lips and stared at John. How could this young person have the temerity to express such opinions when he could know so little? He could not remember expressing an opinion of his own until he was past thirty. He reflected that John's father was probably a Whig!

Colour crept into Mowbray's cheeks, and with effort he managed to keep his temper in check.

'A long speech, my boy. I think that you – and possibly your good father, leading a quiet country life as he must do – may have misunderstood the situation due to a lack of proper information. You must realise that matters appear quite differently when one is in the field. I think that we need to get you into the thick of things, as I have been these many years, to fully appreciate the complexities and the absolute need for non-interference in local customs. I wonder what you have been reading? Nothing, I fear, that will do you much good. A person cannot possibly understand from the perspective of youth and inexperience, or the confines of a parsonage, what it has taken experienced Company men years to learn. As to the management of delicate matters, leave it to those who understand the native mind. We have enough difficulty with the Portuguese and these infernal missionary types pushing their noses into things they know nothing about. I am amazed you were not taught your proper place at Hailey. It is an outrage that we should have to tolerate meddling from people in parsonages who know nothing of the conditions prevailing in the country. No, I say, we should not have to tolerate it. I need to prepare additional material for you, my boy. I see you are come to me already misinformed. You must get off the moralising theme. That tack will not do – no, sir, not at all!'

Mowbray wiped his brow. This young man might be more trouble than he had anticipated. He would need to be closely watched. Reforming poppycock was no good to anyone.

'I hope,' he said, 'that you will be able to be a Company man, John. Remember that morality does not mean the same thing to all men, but all men understand profit. Scruples in these cases can be very expensive.' He drew breath. 'Think carefully. What do you suppose our business is about? And forget politicking.' He finished, and looked expectantly at John.

John felt he had not been properly understood. Mr Mowbray seemed to be extremely cross and had become very red in the face. Deciding to avoid anything to do with traditions and customs, John began carefully.

'I hope I can be of some use, sir. I hope to be useful to the Company and to you. I want to ensure the Company thinks well of me and that I increase my knowledge of its work. I appreciate that I have a great deal to learn. I want to be a credit to my country and my family, to be true to the values I have been taught. If possible, I would like to fit in some painting.'

Mowbray began massaging his temples. He thought of the previous young men placed in his charge.

'I have had an art lover as my assistant before,' he said, looking directly at John. 'He spent hours among the temples and ruins, drawing them by day and by moonlight. He, too, had an eye for the picturesque, and he came to no good.'

Rising, he gestured to the door.

'We will concentrate on the very practical elements of business; the rest will follow. I am an excellent teacher – follow me.'

He led the way out into a closed courtyard. John paused as they made their way past warehouses, marvelling at their size.

'These are nothing, my boy, compared to the magnificent barns at Patna.'

John had heard of these.

'Sir, with respect to our business abroad, I presume from what I have learned that the movement of specific goods of significant value, trade with other nations and superintendence of transport of goods for consumption at home is our core business?'

'Well there,' said Mowbray. 'You make, if I may say so, another error to compound your first! You appear to have accumulated some unusual notions. I must caution you against oversimplification. You need to listen and learn rather than express ill-formed views. No matter, these early difficulties are understandable. How could you appreciate the intricacies? This is why you were entrusted to me. Our business, my boy, is first and foremost to make money for the Company. Secondly, we impose order in the world. Thirdly, to keep the Board informed and our own government advised. We have talked, have we not, about the imperative of non-interference? These are the cornerstones of our policy. We do not interfere, we do not encourage others to interfere, and we punish those who do. We have had to send some missionary types home. There are matters in India which require our administration and judgement, formulation of local laws and suchlike. These are for India's own good. In these matters we must and do interfere.

'This is careful management, a stewardship if you like. I do not want to confuse you with too many minutiae. You must promise to be guided by me in everything for the time being. We will leave it there, except to introduce to you …' – his eyes widened to give added emphasis – '… the vital issues of goods import and goods export'. Mowbray placed a finger to his lips and lowered his voice. 'The vital thing to absorb is that we are not obliged to make all our trading arrangements known to the government of the day. The India Board has managed over the years to accommodate interested parties by careful sifting of information, and long may it continue. There are some in Parliament who have been critical, but they can be managed.

'We need to make sure the people in our area of operations abroad also remain cooperative. It is on this spirit of cooperation that we depend - an "oblige me and I will oblige you" sort of arrangement. We deal in this way with the princes and their peoples. Everyone has a price, if you take my meaning. Of course, we also have a military arm to assist us in maintaining our interests on land and sea, and an increasing number of locally born administrators. I am still not too sure about them. It is usually better if it is our own fellows. Keep them sweet at home by ensuring goods flow homewards and keep the French and Portuguese at bay with the troops. You see,' he continued, wheezing as he leant towards John, 'we Company men know India. She is like the beautiful goddess Khali – lovely to behold, but fickle. We are wary of her particular ways. She is a demanding mistress. We know best, do you see, John?' Mowbray dropped his voice very low. 'The stakes are high. I may say those stakes have nearly killed me. I do not wish to alarm you, but I have been within a hair's breadth of death several times.' He repeated, 'Several times, a hair's breadth. I have told Mrs Mowbray, "do not expect my return. Hope for it, pray for it, but do not expect it".'

John knew that Parliament was taking a close interest in British trade and governance in India. That pressure manifested itself on Mowbray's face, which had turned puce.

'It is a pity that Parliament cannot leave well alone and let us get on with it. Rascals, they know a good thing when they see it and they want a share of the fruits of the pagoda tree for themselves.'

It was as though the mighty task of managing India was Mowbray's alone and he carried the heavy weight of responsibility keenly. Beads of perspiration stood out on his brow. After all, thought John, watching Mr Mowbray mop his forehead, it has nearly killed him. John could sense Mowbray's dedication to duty, but aspects of this concerned him. John did not feel he understood the nature of the business Mr Mowbray described at all. He reasoned that he had misunderstood because of his own lack of experience. Colonel Roberts would never have placed him with an immoral person. John felt somewhat downhearted that his understanding had failed him at the first hurdle.

John was absorbed into the Mowbray household, and was grateful to Mrs Mowbray, who made every effort to make him comfortable. Eve Mowbray was painfully thin and very quiet, and appeared to agree with her husband in everything. She had an abhorrence of rushing about on any pretext.

The two Mowbray daughters were in their late twenties and unmarried. The elder, Adele, ran the household; Bella managed the money. The giggling girls had led John into the cold outer kitchens, where bales of cloth stood against the walls. They said they would let him take some fine muslin for his sisters if he would help them lift the bales out of the house when necessary.

'John, please don't mention this to Father,' Bella explained. 'Going to market is a great secret not to be shared with him, and we do it to help those less fortunate. Not a word to Father, promise me.'

It appeared to be all the girls thought about. There was no pianoforte or singing in the house; sewing baskets were non-existent. Enormous bales of material and parcels would appear in the scullery in the evenings. The girls took them out of the house very early the following day.

Once, when John helped Bella with an unusually large bale of fine muslin, she said, 'We hope, John, that you have not mentioned our works to anyone at all. It will be our little secret. I'm sure you are aware how things are managed in the warehouses. The storeman knows about it, of course, but it must not be described in your letters home. Not everyone would understand.'

John reflected that he would not have known about their works at all if they had not told him about the bolts of material in the back scullery. He could not understand why they appeared to want to take him into their confidence.

John was used to his sisters helping those less fortunate in the village but he struggled to see what the poor would do with bales of silk. He wondered why the girls could not discuss the matter openly with their father. It was surely a good thing to help the poor of the district. John found the general requirement for secrecy within the house unsettling. It seemed to apply to the most trivial of things, even the consumption of candles and foodstuffs. The girls did not always speak respectfully about their father, which also made John uncomfortable. They appeared to take little notice of their mother when she asked them to do the smallest of things, and John found himself helping Mrs Mowbray when he could.

Despite a pervading sense of anxiety which he could not explain, John settled into the routine of home and office. He spent his days looking over Mr Mowbray's rounded shoulders at the many ledgers and accounts. These accounts and reports detailed the export of iron, wood, cloth, gum, bullets, rope, and tools, various; and the costs of pottery, ships' sailcloth, servants' wages, decent horses, fodder for elephants, and saltpetre. The range and quantity of goods was astonishing. He came to see the crucial importance of exports of British manufacture to India and the care required to safeguard imports of tea and silk. He felt sure that the East India Company had been very keen to support the move to abolish slavery but that there were complexities. The Company would prefer that the plantation owners should stand on their own two feet. Indian trade suffered because of free labour in the Americas and the Caribbean. Mowbray pointed to an entry.

'I would like to see the plantation owners try to make a profit against such competition. If it were not for the determination of men such as me, where would we be? The Company has reason to be grateful to me, John.'

John made a mental note to send this news home. It was important to him that his parents knew he was working for a right-thinking man. However, he would avoid Mr Mowbray's opinion on the matter of slavery. John unrolled a map of India with vast areas in pink indicating the Company-controlled provinces. Mr Mowbray pointed to those regions that caused the most trouble. It was his view that most of the Indian princes were unpredictable.

'Ordinary workers in India do not expect much consideration. Prices are kept low if the headmen are managed properly. The princes, though, are another matter. Riches beyond imagining, and the starving at their gate, but the Company needs them.'

At dinner that evening, John suggested that it might be helpful to consider the feelings that British control must engender in any proud prince who found himself accountable to outside influence. This was not well received. John began to wonder if he was pleasing Mr Mowbray in any regard.

The following morning, Mowbray did not appear at breakfast. John received a message to go straight to Blackwall once he was dressed. In the office there was an unusual amount of bustle. A flushed and wheezing Mowbray appeared through a low doorway.

'Packing cases, my boy – we need 'em. Pack everything you have, for the insects will have at least half of your linen before a month is out.'

John stared at the pile of goods in the middle of the floor.

'Are you to travel, sir?'

'Yes, for heaven's sake, John – we both are! Be careful of the boxes – do not step there. I really don't know what to do first. I have made sure we are in the roundhouse cabin because I have been in the Great Cabin and it is sheer purgatory. We are off, my boy, so unexpectedly, and this time I will be killed for sure. We do not go to Lahore but to Calcutta, which can be very nasty at any time of year. I have told Mrs Mowbray I am needed by the Company abroad to manage the Chinese and that I will not be returning home. Where the Indian has failed to kill me, the Chinese will surely succeed. I have, of course, some experience with them and these things are remembered by our superiors.' He pointed skywards. 'I flatter myself that I am well thought of as a capable and experienced manager. To be called upon in certain delicate negotiations is something indeed. I am flattered. I really am. But I have talked long enough, and there is little time.'

Shaking a sheaf of papers at John, he closed one eye.

'John, these papers I have in my hand are secret dispatches.' He paused, dissatisfied by the effect of his announcement on John. He lowered his voice to a whisper, glancing about him. 'We must do our duty whatever the personal risk. We leave in less than one week. We need to arrange for every stick of furniture we will need on board ship. The roundhouse cabin is a bare-board affair only. We shall need our cots and a writing table, chests and seating. I will have a tarpaulin and a washbasin this time, and my cushions. I cannot overemphasise the need for home comforts on such a voyage. I cannot exaggerate the urgency. They have arranged special passage on the ship for me.'

Shouting loudly and perspiring, Mowbray ran up and down the corridors of the offices all day, so that nobody could be in doubt of the importance of his forthcoming voyage or its purpose and by the end of the day no secrets remained.

He was heard loudly requisitioning a water filter, candles, and a quantity of small arms in case of pirates. John was sent on a hundred errands, and at day's end he could not say that he was any clearer about their reason for going. That evening, Mrs Mowbray could just be heard telling her daughters in her softest voice that this rushing about would be the death of their father. John noticed that, although many hankies were pressed to noses, very few tears were shed by any of the Mowbray ladies when they came to say goodbye.

The fleet of fifteen ships stood at anchor in East India Docks. There would be no time for John's family to write more than a few lines containing their love and good wishes. These were delivered by Colonel Roberts and Reverend Deuchars, who met John for a subdued meal before the ship sailed. John's father seemed particularly quiet. His last words to his son were difficult to bear. Despite John's reassurance that he was the best of fathers, Edward Deuchars apologised tearfully to his son for being unable to keep him at home. He said that the thought of him going so far away was unbearable, and he wept for the necessity of it. John had never seen his father this distressed; he was so used to his hope and optimism. He tried to reassure his father that they had always talked so positively about his future and this was just the chance they had hoped for to make use of all he had been taught. For all that, Edward would not be comforted. Held up by his stepbrother, he managed to address John.

'I would have wished to keep you at home but, because I was such a stubborn young man, my children's futures are uncertain. I will never forgive myself. I hope you are more successful than I have been and that you can forgive me, John. I love you. God bless you and keep you.'

John clasped his father's hand.

'Father, your example is what I will aspire to daily. I would wish you to be proud of me. Look after Mother and the girls until I return.'

Edward Deuchars held his son close, kissed him, and pressed several letters from home into his hands along with a small leather pouch containing all the money he could spare. Then he walked quickly away. John shook his uncle's hand and thanked him for all he had done. He stood and watched until his father and the Colonel were both out of sight. Neither of the men turned to wave.

Later, John watched the small cockboats unloading trunks and fellow travellers' goods and possessions onto the East Indiamen. His own few things were among them, including the letters, the small pouch and something more substantial from the Colonel. It all felt so sudden, so final. He was leaving everyone dear to him, and for first time he began to consider that he might never come home. Then he remembered Helen. She had dared him to leave without her. How could she have imagined any other course?

The ship sailed with the ebb tide on a clear morning in February 1829. John thought of his parting on the quayside. He wished that this last memory was not one of his beloved father's weeping. But there it was – he could not alter it. He also recalled Mrs Mowbray's strangeness as they had parted. She looked earnestly into his eyes and, holding tightly onto his sleeve, whispered something to him. He thought he must have imagined it, but he was sure she had said something about taking great care to avoid the perfect flower. John could not think what she meant.

Chapter Three

The first days of the voyage in the *New Devonshire* were not kind to its passengers. John was seasick and, despite their reasonably comfortable accommodation in the roundhouse cabin, being confined in cramped conditions with Hugh Mowbray was unpleasant. He pitied the poor wretches in the accommodation on the lower decks – at least he had some daylight and air. Once the severe nausea diminished, he might have found conditions manageable. The constant sound of marching feet above his head and the proximity of the poulterer made rest impossible. For the first two weeks, the ships were within sight of each other and their naval escort, which was comforting. Mowbray was in excellent health and able to enjoy the very reasonable fare offered at the Captain's table. He saw no need for John to accompany him, but always recounted exactly what the Captain had said to him by way of compliments so that, as Mr Mowbray said, 'the invalid should not miss out'.

He told John he was extremely gratified that the Captain had found his hints about the route taken on his previous voyage useful. He was also at pains to establish that the Captain was carefully following the Company hydrographer's recommendations and detailed nautical charts. There is no record of how the Captain received these attempts at navigational assistance. It was, however, made very clear that Mowbray's particular attention was not required in relation to the correctness of procedure and timing of the deck exercises. These were performed by a small group of marines under the Captain's reproving eye. Mowbray had better luck with the chaplain, who seemed only too glad of his suggestions for appropriate biblical texts to be used in the Sunday services on deck.

John emerged from the cabin feeling sickly and unsteady on his feet. He had come up on deck out of absolute necessity. Mr Mowbray was a continual talker. All the window panes were closed, but the rough conditions had taken a toll on bedding and carpets inside the roundhouse. Once on deck, John looked out at the rolling green sea, watching the gobbets of froth blowing about on the slippery wood. He looked at the poor fellows heaving at ropes which held the huge sails. His soaking feet left the deck as he walked, almost as if he was floating. Then, just as quickly, his knees sank beneath him as the ship shuddered, cracking like a walnut against each wave. Somebody pushed past and growled at him to get below. It was one of the junior officers. These men had been so courteous when the passengers had boarded, but in rough conditions they cursed them.

The sailors were fighting to bring in sail in worsening conditions. John could hear a cow bellowing her protest into the wind somewhere starboard. In need of peace and some relief from the tossing deck, he found a quiet corner behind the partitioned cabins. He began a letter in pencil to his mother, meaning to enclose one or two sketches of the ship, but these remained unfinished on account of his feeling so ill. It had been difficult to stay upright on deck but sitting crouching over a letter made him feel worse. He put away his papers, fearful that the scrawled mess would alarm rather than reassure his mother.

Mowbray tried to encourage him to eat. As this was a voyage of months, he had to try something while the food was reasonable. Mowbray had already talked to the galley at length about appropriate fare for invalids at sea, and had encouraged John to use some of the resources provided by the Colonel to secure them a better breakfast.

John heard the officers bemoaning the fact that the fleet had become separated due to the bad weather. It was with relief that, after eight weeks, two of the ships were sighted off the coast of Madagascar. The respite was short lived, however. That evening John noticed determined preparations both on deck and below. The cargo of Lancashire cloth in its sailcloth bales, timber, iron and other British goods was fastened tight for fear of shifting. All the poultry and the cow were taken below protesting, and the deck was eerily empty of debris. The crew became unnaturally quiet in their work, and flags which John did not recognise were hauled up and down the masts of the sister ships. Mowbray's outrage at a very poor dinner was heard throughout the ship.

John felt uneasy but, on applying to Mr Mowbray, he was told not to speak of any matter relating to possible misfortune at sea. It was not the 'done thing'. The storm hit in the middle of that night. The wind howled in the rigging, and the ship cracked and groaned as if it would splinter. The storm was of such intensity that John was sure they could not survive, but his seasickness left him completely. Lightning illuminated the rigging and the whole sky seemed to be on fire. John peered through a crack in the partition that gave out onto stairs leading to the poop deck. He listened to the howling of the wind and the crashing waves. Rain and spray were pouring down the stairs. He felt that at any moment the ship would be filled completely with water. The door of the cabin flew open, lamps were extinguished and everything went as black as pitch. Suddenly bolts of lightning lit up the confined space. Mr Mowbray lay in his bunk, hands clasped together as if in prayer. In the flashes of lightning, John thought he saw a figure in the stairwell outside their cabin. He could hear the waves crashing onto the deck above but could not imagine why anyone would be out in the open in such weather. John knew it would be foolhardy to go out into the storm, but he leant out of the doorway and shouted a warning. He was certain he could see a man standing against the bulwark at the top of the short flight of steps. The figure paused to steady himself, hands either side of a narrow door. John shouted again. Mr Mowbray, terrified, called to

John to come in and shut the cabin door, but John clasped his wet-weather topcoat around him and made for the stairs.

The ship lurched, throwing itself wildly from side to side as if trying to shake off the sea. It seemed to plunge downwards, shuddering to a standstill against each crashing wave. As he stepped into the narrow space leading to the main deck, he was knocked off his feet by a wall of water. It swept over him and down the wooden steps behind. He was hurled into the outer rail, which took away all his breath. The force of the water pinned him fast. It was dark, and the ship rolled and dipped, throwing him forward onto his outstretched hands. The next wave was so powerful that it slammed his face into the planking. Instantly another wave washed over him and he felt he could not breathe. The wind screamed in the rigging as the water swept him across the deck. It was as if the sea meant to take him.

He crawled on his hands and knees, fingernails scratching at the deck for any hold. He looked up as another bolt of lightning illuminated the rigging and a wall of water hit him hard, rolling him close to the rail. The water receded and he found himself fast against the gunwale, level with the raging sea. He could hardly bear to move again. Pain coursed through his side, his face stung and he began to shake with shock and cold. As more lightning blazed across the sky, John could just make out a crouched figure lying across a raised hatch cover not far ahead of him. The man was clutching a rope fastened across the hatch. John knew that his only chance was to reach the crouched figure and the comparative safety of the hatch cover. He also knew that it would be impossible to stand upright. He crawled slowly across the deck, deluged with water each time the ship plunged into the waves. Somehow he managed to make his way forward. He could see the crew wholly absorbed in keeping the ship afloat, nobody moving to help him.

John was exhausted but made a final lunge at the crouched figure. As the next wave crashed onto the deck he rolled over the top of the hatch. He found himself holding on to the stranger's soaking coat. He manoeuvred until he covered the still form with his own body. He wedged himself behind the unconscious man and the hatch cover, fastening his outstretched fingers into the ironwork grille. There was no way back – they would have to wait out the storm until help arrived. His face pressed against the cold flesh of his anonymous companion, John was soaked through to the bone. The noise of the wind was deafening and salt water stung his face. John looked up and saw another wave coming towards the ship, and closed his eyes. This wave did not strike as the others had done. Instead, he felt the ship being heaved upwards. He opened his eyes and looked through the rain and spray to the horizon. The ship seemed to hang momentarily on top of the green tumult. He thought he saw a light in the distance, then felt the ship pitch downwards; John stared horrified into the deep green void.

He could not tell how far down they went, sliding, groaning, into the dark valley of water. He could not believe they could survive, and everything seemed to slow. He could feel the deck strain under him. He kept his eyes open – what more was there to fear now? The silent and terrible wall of water rose up around the ship. John watched as it shuddered in the interminable slide to the bottom. He thought they must be at least forty feet down. He prayed and resigned himself to death. He had no idea how long he lay there, the green water raging on either side, but somehow it did not touch him. It grew quiet and he watched as the water seemed to enclose him. There was a quiet finality about it all. His only regret was that he had been unable to see his mother to say goodbye.

He felt an intense coldness, rushing salt air on his face, pressure against his body. He tried to breathe. It was as if something was trying to crush all life. He would arrive in the deeps infinitesimally small, like a grain of sand. This is how sand is made, everything crushed into tiny pieces. It seemed to become light; he saw everything shimmering and was awed by the terrible beauty. John saw himself in the conservatory at the Parsonage, a fire blazing at one end. His mother was sitting, head bowed over her book, but she could not hear him calling although he screamed her name. Huge plants slapped and clawed at his face. Each leaf dripped a blue liquid into small bottles, which he kicked away but they kept rolling back towards him. The floor of the conservatory was slippery. He held on to the branches of the trees until his arms ached. He knew he must avoid falling among the shining blue bottles. He knew he must not let go of the branches. His mother looked up at him and smiled.

It was a little after dawn that the wind dropped and the sea grew calmer. John felt himself being lifted. He felt his head bang against the solid teak doorway. He woke shivering in his soaking cot. His head ached and he could not feel his arms. He struggled to open his eyes, with limited success. A shadow passed before him and he could hear the murmur of voices. He attempted to speak but his throat was thick and tight, and no sound came. Fellow passengers feared for the life of young John Deuchars, but he was talked about as the hero of the night. It was said that Mr Thomas Row owed him his life.

The passengers spoke of the missing bowsprit, snapped clean off in the storm, for at least a week afterwards. Everyone watched the ship's carpenter skilfully fashion another to take its place. In a tedious journey and after such deliverance, diversions were most welcome. They were a safe alternative to contemplation of near death. Mowbray spared no effort in making sure of John's recovery. He accompanied the Ship's Surgeon in every consultation, offering his opinion as to what could be done. He recommended warm draughts of salt beef tea, plasters and a bleeding regimen. He produced recipes for remedies whose ingredients were not to be found on board. Mowbray made it very clear that leeches should have been carried on board.

The fuss about the leeches did it. Pushed beyond endurance, the Surgeon showed Mowbray the door. John had been placed in a cabin with windows on the poop deck. Mowbray said he would have much preferred his cot in the roundhouse, especially as most of his own furniture had been rendered matchwood by the storm. Mowbray was telling John plaintively that the sea had tossed some very lovely inlaid pieces about his cabin until every chair was missing a leg and his stores lay in a sodden mess. He did not spare John any detail and was just telling him, for the third time, that all his lovely blue china washing bowls were in pieces and linen ruined, when he was removed and told not to return without the Surgeon's permission. Mowbray was furious. In earlier, less straitened, times he would have booked his passage on the poop deck as a matter of course. Mowbray considered that John had recovered well enough and he thought it unseemly that John, as his assistant, should remain in more comfort than he. The Surgeon would hear none of it.

Fellow passengers were not disposed to offer appropriate sympathy either. Mowbray fancied himself ill-used. He was unimpressed when told by the other passengers that the man saved, Thomas Row, was an aspiring young lawyer recently jilted by a fiancée unwilling to leave her family and make the journey to India. His only consolation was a return to India to take up a more senior position. Mowbray was completely unmoved. The law had nearly cost him a valuable assistant whose fingers would surely never be as agile as they might have been. This fuss was extremely galling, young lawyers being two a penny. Row would hardly have been missed, and to console himself Mowbray purchased some essentials from the purser with John's allowance in anticipation of John's recovery. The washing bowl and dry linen was some consolation.

Separation from Mr Mowbray was the turning point. John was young and strong. After four weeks he took his first steps on a very different deck. Mercifully, the only excitements during the remaining voyage were flying fish. They made the ladies squeal as they hurled themselves onto the ship. It was suspected that they accounted for the rather strange flavour of the soup at dinner.

After five months at sea, the ship reached the Maldives, where the captain secured supplies. To everyone's relief they found some of their sister ships in port. The harbour was teeming with life, the colour, noise and fragrances all new to John. Impossible meats were cooking in the open air. There were bright delicacies on huge plates. Vendors held dishes precariously high above their heads as they pushed through the crowds. There were piles of goods on the dockside ready to be loaded, and so many people jostling and shouting, some brightly robed. There were merchants in tense negotiations screaming to be heard above the noise. Sailors spilled out of taverns. It was John's first taste of the East. He was amazed by the rich dress, the splendidly decorated buildings and the strange, fragrant foods. Not completely recovered from his experiences at sea, he found himself gagging as rich, spice-laden smells wafted past him.

He passed a legless beggar, covered in flies, squinting up at him in the hot sun. Women surrounded him with their children, calling to him in a language he did not understand. John instinctively pulled away from the filthy, hollow-eyed urchins who tugged at his coats and spat at him when he gave them nothing. He suddenly felt unable to cope with the noise and clamour. He had no energy and little remaining money. The heat burned into his clothes, but he knew he could not appear to falter in front of Mr Mowbray.

Coming into port gave leisure for Mowbray to talk to John about their arrangements on arrival in Calcutta. He was relieved by John's recovery and began to talk of the future.

'We will be met by Sir Josiah Coatsworth. You will have heard of him, of course?' John had not. 'He is the new Home Secretary in Bengal, reporting to the Governor-General, who in turn is answerable to the Court of Directors in London. He is to assist us on our arrival. He should have advanced further, as should I, but only influence will secure governorships. They say he has done very well for himself given his humble beginnings. They also say he is Governor-General in name only. After all, what would an aristocrat know about India? Our new Governor-General consults Sir Josiah in everything. We must make ourselves agreeable to him.'

This description of Sir Josiah's new status was probably overblown. It suited Mowbray to think of himself in close proximity to that most revered personage, the Governor-General.

'Sir Josiah has been in India for many years,' Mowbray continued, 'and some people think that he richly deserves his position. He has a family, with a daughter, Julia – a very lovely girl of about sixteen. When I last saw her, she had the makings of a very lovely woman. If I recall correctly, she has a magnificent mane of blonde hair and the most striking eyes.'

Mowbray paused and coughed, quickly turning the conversation in another direction.

'It is out with the old and in with the new, my boy. They will need experience and I have plenty of that. I have been advised to proceed to Calcutta and later to Patna. We are to tread a familiar road – familiar to me, you understand. As Factory Superintendent I am to advise the presidency at Fort William on the exact state regarding the precious bloom – "the perfect flower" – which is so essential in maintaining essential supplies of other very valuable goods.'

As Mr Mowbray spoke, he stroked a waistcoat of very richly embroidered cloth. A question was forming in John's mind, but he did not pursue it because he had learned to be careful about what he asked.

'We are used to our teas, are we not?' Mowbray continued. 'His Majesty must have only the very best tea.' He paused and looked very seriously at John. 'We have had reports of some very serious lapses in security in our factories in Patna. I am to superintend some rigorous procedures before and following the harvest. I am to see to the better management of all things in Calcutta and Patna. Naturally, you will assist me – you are, after all, the junior assistant factory superintendent.'

Suddenly, Mowbray spun round on his short legs.

'I cannot believe I have not made sure of this before. You are under twenty-five, are you not? The Opium Manual will not allow you to be a day older.'

John replied that he was indeed under twenty-five.

'Well, it would have been a serious oversight had you been older. I would have had to send you back immediately. There was a very excellent fellow,' mused Mowbray, 'whom I brought out here on my last tour. India killed him dead. He flung himself into the arms of Morpheus, foolish boy. There was absolutely nothing I could do, although of course I did my best. He was but twenty-four years old and should have known better.'

John was aware of feeling suddenly cold, which given the July temperature was unusual. He put it down to his recent illness, which had sapped his strength.

'Am I to understand, sir, that we are not to be involved in matters relating to tea?' he asked.

Mowbray looked hard at John. He now had serious concerns about this boy, Deuchars. Had he not explained at length the Company's business? It should be crystal clear to this youth, but he was determined to be stupid! He felt he had made sufficient allowance for the quantities of sea water John had swallowed, but now he must recover.

'No, dear boy, we are not.' He was irritated. 'The case regarding the perfect flower is far more important than tea. Without the poppy there would be no tea! I have already explained all this to you at some length in the last months, but you have not been attending. This must be due to your accident, which I must say has been inconvenient.' He paused. 'Don't worry, I will keep you right – Colonel Roberts would expect nothing less. I will tell you something of our Patna operation later, when you are feeling stronger. You must know that everything is the last word in efficiency of manufacture. It is an enormous enterprise.'

Forgetting John's fatigue, he continued, 'The native workers are a model of organisation, so happy in their occupation. The Company is very careful with them because they are craftsmen, and craftsmen take time to reach perfection in their skill. I have said many times to members of the India Board in London that I believe in starting them young and I think this has been taken up. I see them younger at each visit.'

'Mr Mowbray, sir,' persisted John, 'I understand we have need of morphia, but why in such enormous quantities?'

'You know,' said Mr Mowbray, looking sideways at John, not trusting his temper, 'I have explained that we are entering a new age. Everything is done in large quantities for the expanding marketplace. This is growth, boy, and it's all a question of … Oh, never mind! I think that is quite enough for now. We will talk in more detail another day. I have worked hard enough in this humidity. I give you the benefit of my experience free and gratis. I prepare each advisory treatise in my mind before delivery, it quite exhausts me.' He was perspiring heavily as he continued. 'You must husband your health or India will enervate you. But I am pleased you are feeling so much better after your little setback. We will leave off business for today. Now do go, my dear boy, and see about our dinner.' Mowbray pointed to a distant house which leant against the wall at the farthest end of the port gate. 'It's not far; the walk will do you good!'

Chapter Four

The ship made its way into the Hooghly River from the vastness of the Bay of Bengal. John knew that he would not be overseeing the production of tea. His role was not to tame the dangerous northern provinces to consolidate British interests. He would not be negotiating with a bored prince from a comfortable office in Calcutta. Instead, he would be an opium inspector, watching over – what did Mr Mowbray call it? – the perfect flower. John had wanted an adventure, to play some part in the huge changes that he saw at work in the world. He had studied hard at Hailey and imagined going to India to make his fortune and to improve his family's circumstances. Now, here he was, and he must make the most of the chance he had been given.

The world was changing; he knew that his father and uncle at home were concerned at the encroachment of industry on the land bordering Deerfield. There seemed to be chimneys of some sort or other on every horizon, which John found exciting. He had friends who were sons of mine-owners; if there was money in it, what was wrong with that? His own grandfather had been a mining engineer. This was perhaps the only source of dissent at home. He and his father did not agree on the nature of the new spirit of enterprise. John saw the change as progress, while his father saw it as the bringer of evils of various sorts.

His father's parish included the cottages of lead miners, and the effects of alcohol and disease in those places were the cause of much concern at the Parsonage. Lead mining was hard – something about the stuff worked on the constitution until it rotted a man away from the inside. There was no medicine which a worker could afford when illness struck. John thought that conditions needed to improve but that the industrial process itself was absolutely essential. He knew of the use of opium in medicine and its pain-relieving properties, but had not realised just how valuable a commodity it was. Mr Mowbray's explanation of the opium trade had not been clear. John made up his mind to learn more; it was important he did not look foolish.

It did seem that most of Mr Mowbray's explanations were rather obscure. John was getting used to this. He would have asked his father for clarification if he had been able. He attempted to rationalise in his own mind the events of the last months and the effects of his own illness. He thought aloud: 'I am unnerved, that is all. I am at a distance from home. I must face these challenges with a positive spirit. My future will be bright, my prospects good – why should they not be?'

John made up his mind to look again at the papers given to him by Mr Mowbray detailing the regulation and work of the factory. He was determined to read and understand all one hundred and ninety-five forms relating to the management of opium in Patna. He had promised to be an able assistant to Mr Mowbray and he meant to keep his word.

They reached Calcutta as darkness fell on the hot and humid evening of 5th August 1829. The outline of Fort William was barely visible against the darkening sky.

'There will be a thunderstorm for sure,' said Mr Mowbray. 'We have arrived in the nick of time.' He mopped his brow. 'This can a very sticky time of year, but it is not as hot as it will be in the next months, my boy.'

They were met with their trunks and other luggage, and taken by rickshaw through narrow alleyways past low dwellings. The air was stifling and raised voices could be heard through doorways. Not a creature stirred outside; John had expected crowds but there were none. Mr Mowbray, sensing some disappointment, spoke.

'Oh, but wait, John, until you have seen the palaces. Wait until you have seen inside the Fort and Belvedere House, the Governor-General's residence. I have been invited to most of the grand ones, you know.'

John had been told this many times, and it was true the houses they now passed were impressive. Eventually the carriage slowed and they pulled into a narrow lane and entered a courtyard. Mowbray clapped his hands.

'There is no greater treasure than good servants!'

A door in the building opened and a very tall, turbaned man stepped out and bowed low.

'Ah, Mukherjee. Still here, I see. Now take these things inside and be so kind as to show us to our rooms.'

Mowbray took John's arm and pushed him forward.

'Yes, thank you, Mukherjee, move along now and for the Lord's sake let us get inside.'

The big house was cool. John could swear he could hear birds singing. The sound echoed in the darkness of a massive hall.

After washing and changing they were led into a candlelit room with a red-tiled floor. It was filled with the most exotic plants with broad green leaves. The birdsong was now explained, as vivid blue-and-yellow songbirds fluttered in the high-ceilinged room. Disturbed, they were flying from branch to branch like movable blooms. In one corner, there appeared to be a statue, until he moved. The man was dressed in white; he wore a turban and a gold sash slung at the waist in which hung a shining scimitar. At the far side of the room a table was covered with plates and glassware. It looked as if a meal were about to be served. John recalled his aunt's dinner table on Old Year's Night, when the finest things were set out. There were large tureens of fruit at either end of the table, a fireplace on one wall and massive ferns spread around. The whole room appeared as if it were half in and half out of a large garden.

Huge cabinets of ornately carved Indian rosewood, packed full of blue china, lined the nearside walls. Chairs made of rattan and covered in orange damask were placed either side of the fireplace. Golden birds craned their necks into the shimmering centre of the ornate cushions. A large sofa in the most exquisite green-and-gold silk was situated in the middle of the room. The curtains at each side of the doors at one end of the room were of rich green-and-bronze silk. At first glance, it seemed an English country scene – until John noticed carvings of elephants. On the floor in front of the hearth was the most enormous tiger skin and above the fireplace a pair of muskets.

John was about to bend towards the tiger skin to look closely at the animal's large teeth when footsteps clicked on the tiled floor. A tall man in what looked like morning dress came marching through the wide arched doorway. He was dressed in a jacket and cravat but around his legs he wore white pantaloons. His feet were encased in gold-and-black slippers.

'Mowbray – about time! What kept you, man? We have a crisis. I asked for someone months ago. Where on earth have you been? The harvest is in the making already. Naturally you will know that, as you are one of the old hands. They keep sending me old men and boys, damn boys!' His tone was clipped and impatient. 'I see you have one here.' The man paced up to John and looked closely at him. 'Who are you, sir?'

'I'm so sorry,' said Mowbray. 'I do beg your pardon, Sir Josiah. May I introduce Mr John Deuchars, who is presently assisting me at the request of Colonel Roberts, who –'

'Yes, I know Roberts!' boomed Sir Joshua Coatsworth. 'A good man in a tight spot. A pity they did not send him!' He turned to John. 'Are you any relation to the Newcastle Deuchars? Distantly, I expect. I hope you are stronger than your predecessor. Did the army reject you? Only fit occupation for a young man, you know, the army, I say.' Back to Mowbray. 'I take it he knows why he's here, Mowbray? It's a bloody mess, a damn inconvenient and bloody mess!'

Mowbray, perspiring heavily, had opened his mouth but had not been able to interrupt. Sir Josiah, cool in his immaculate ensemble, looked upon his visitors and frowned.

'Sit down. Not on the silk! Sit down *there*, will you?'

It was an order rather than a request. Sir Josiah clicked his fingers. This, thought John, was not a man to waste time. Nervous energy accompanied his every movement. Sir Josiah looked at him.

'I will need to interview you properly, young man, in order to decide if there is any point in your going north. There is nothing to be gained if you are not useful. You look very young and not a little ill to me. Return here in two days at eight-thirty precisely in the morning. Do not be late – I abhor lateness!'

Mowbray opened his mouth again to advise Sir Josiah that they were supposed to be staying with him, but thought better of it. There was movement in the direction of a decorated arched doorway. John turned, relieved at the distraction. A young woman in an orange-and-gold costume appeared. Her dress completely covered her but was no disguise for her lovely figure. She walked barefoot into the room bearing a large silver plate on which sat a very English-looking teapot and a large sugar basin. Her eyes were fixed to the floor. Almost immediately another girl followed, dressed in a light-blue sari of the same design. John wondered at two servants to bring in one tea tray.

Sir Josiah turned and, with a loud snort, said, 'You fooled 'em, my dear! Gentlemen, this is my daughter, Julia. She will look after you here tonight.'

The girl in the blue sari looked directly at John and unwound her headdress. She was graceful and her hair of gold curled into a plait as thick as a man's wrist. The coil fell down her back, small curls clustered around her brow. She had large, ice-blue eyes and a beautiful smile. She waved her hand and the orange sari disappeared.

'We find in hot weather that it is so much more comfortable to wear these loose-fitting clothes at home. I see you find me quite shocking, most of the new arrivals do. We find ourselves quite at odds with the new face of Calcutta society. It is becoming quite a little England.'

She waited for an answer but John could think of none, so she continued.

'Tell me, has India caused you many surprises since your arrival?'

John was tongue-tied. He had never seen such beauty – she was perfect. Her hair was astonishing and he had to control a strong desire to touch it.

Julia's hands were tiny, her fingers covered in rings. One in particular caught his eye; it was gold, set with a large ruby which caught the light. It appeared to burn. Finding his tongue, he told her they had just arrived and asked when she had come out to India. This produced a peal of laughter.

'I have been here for ever! I have lived in India almost my whole life – never went home, as would have been proper. I was a very determined small child and refused to go. I speak two dialects well and one badly. I dance and sing in the traditional way my ayah taught me in the days when nobody could think it was shocking. Now everything about me is regarded by some as shocking. I do not think that the ladies who come fresh from England approve of us at all. They must be careful – new arrivals cannot upset the Superintendent's daughter. Of course, I dress conventionally when I go out to promenade, or receive calls, but at home we dress to keep cool, as would anyone with sense.'

John thought her dress practical and *in the privacy of one's own home, who could object?* Indeed, *who would object to anything she did?* Julia was pleased to meet a person closer to her own age, as new personalities were valuable in a restricted social circle. She was determined to make the most of the visit.

Mowbray and Sir Josiah had moved away together across the long room. This allowed Julia and John to converse privately. John found himself talking about his home, his family and how difficult the voyage had been. Julia realised that John missed his family at home very much and was charmed by his devotion to his sisters. She felt able to confide in him.

'I have no idea what "home" as you describe it is like, you know. I cannot remember much about England. I remember tall, dark buildings and grey skies. Most of my memories are of here in India, with its colour, light and life. Calcutta is wonderful and exciting. I don't think I could be persuaded to go home – that is, to England. If I did, I am sure they would exhibit me as a curiosity. I would need very good reasons to leave this place.'

John thought of the reaction she might provoke in some quarters in England. He was also sure that, should any insult to this lovely girl be attempted in his presence, he would defend her with his life.

'It is strange,' Julia went on, 'that the ladies who come out are nearly killed by the heat and the insects, and cannot wait to leave. It is because they compare India to England; they make no allowances in their habits, nor dress for the climate. They are uncomfortable and frequently ill. If you will permit me to give you some early advice, it is to be kind to your servants and adapt as quickly as possible in your clothes and routines. You will be so much more comfortable and healthier if you do.'

John was aware that, on the other side of the room, Sir Josiah was doing most of the talking. He had Mr Mowbray firmly by the elbow and very deliberately moved him towards the large arched doors. The men were not quite out of earshot and could be heard above the sound of birdsong.

John heard Sir Josiah say that affairs were worse than previously thought. That 'Malwa' opium from the princely states was undercutting the produce from Patna. He heard something about slackness in the factory. He noticed that Sir Josiah had placed his long index finger on the breast of Mr Mowbray's lovely waistcoat. He emphasised his concerns by prodding Mr Mowbray's heaving chest. Sir Josiah was saying something about 'the wretched raiders', whoever they were. Julia turned to John, aware of the impropriety, and apologised.

'They go to business quickly because things are not as they should be, but you have come to put it all right,' she said, smiling at him.

He told her that he was determined to do well. It seemed to him that he could tell this lovely creature anything, that he had known her always. They even exchanged a few words in Urdu. John thought that he might have impressed her, but her skills were far in advance of his. She seemed interested in his preparations for his work and said she thought his knowledge of languages would be most useful. John wanted her to continue to talk to him, as he wanted to hear more about her.

Sir Josiah suddenly wheeled around, satisfied that he had made himself crystal clear to Mowbray.

'Refreshments, gentlemen!' he exclaimed, 'and afterwards my daughter might play a little something for us. Julia is an accomplished harpist, without question the best we have here in Calcutta.'

Sir Josiah was a convivial host. Over tea he spoke of the poppy-growing in the north and of the need to treat carefully with the Chinese who purchased the opium manufactured at Patna via intermediaries. He described the huge barns called godowns, in which the poppy 'cakes' were made. His hands moved slowly and delicately as he described how the cakes were prepared. He spoke to John about the skill of the workers.

'The poppy is beautiful when in bud, all softness just before it opens. When the flower blooms there is no perfume like it. It is a fragrance which can carry one quite away. They place the refined opium gently at the very centre of the "cake" and then cover it over and over with petals from the poppy flower. The Chinese love it, in fact they cannot get enough. It's just like tobacco there – everyone uses it.

'Sadly,' he continued, 'the Qing Emperor has become a little sensitive, for some reason. So we must be careful. We do not sell to the Chinese directly, but through factors and others who see it through to its final destination. It appears that we can no longer supply the product via our own people. I feel we should do as we please. The diplomats, as ever, hold sway, hence it is important to ensure there are no problems which could embarrass His Majesty's Government. There are already those in Parliament who seek to undermine the position of the Company – the same people who would like to see us brought to heel, and that would never do. We could not achieve half as much in India without the income from the perfect flower.'

With Sir Josiah's calm, reasoned explanation, John felt that he had a clearer idea about the whole business. He could now see that all he was required to do was to assist in the administration and movement of the goods. The Chinese depended upon opium and he would make sure they got it. He wished it could have been explained in this way much earlier; perhaps he would not have worried quite so much.

While drinking hot, sweet tea, John listened to Julia at the harp. As she played, a delicious sound echoed within the room. Her gown of gossamer-fine silk rippled as she stroked the strings; it was if her whole person trembled. Then she was still, her head bowed, hands across the strings, holding them fast in her tiny hands.

After dinner, John and Mowbray walked down the massive stone steps of the mansion to their accommodation. The older man was quieter than usual.

'Well,' he said, 'I do think they could have made room for us in the main house. It is a trial to have to shift about like this after such a long journey! I am glad that interview with Sir Josiah is over and our real work can begin. How do you like it, my boy? I must say, I think they are pretty relieved that I have come. Did you notice how much Sir Josiah had to say to me? It is always gratifying when one is consulted in that way – such attention to detail and even refreshments laid out for me. Sir Josiah is relieved because he knows I am at his right hand. He has been a personal friend and colleague to me for some years. I am sure I must have mentioned this to you.'

Mowbray then talked of Sir Josiah's plant collection.

'I imagine that your mother would be delighted to receive one of those huge floral specimens for her hothouse. I told Sir Josiah several times that he had a most wonderful collection of orchids. They would please even Mr Scott, I think. I refer to the Company's botanist, you know. Now you might try and draw one or two of those, John. I have to admit that you are talented with those pencils of yours.'

Mowbray's red silk waistcoat rose and fell. Large droplets of perspiration spilled onto the intertwining birds and flowers. As they soaked in to the shining fabric, it looked as if Mowbray was bleeding. John instinctively took out the clean handkerchief he had discreetly retrieved from his portmanteau. It had two large holes in it. Mr Mowbray glanced at it and shook his head slowly from side to side.

'I warned you about insects, did I not?'

But John was not listening. His thoughts were of that shining creature with the most beautiful voice he had ever heard. Julia Coatsworth, a perfect girl who surely would not look twice at a man with holes in his handkerchief!

John was proved wrong. In the three weeks before his departure to the north, he was invited to Sir Josiah's home each day. Julia and John sat in the shady summerhouse drinking sweet tea, speaking in dialect and drawing a little. Julia played her harp for him beautifully while he drew her portrait. By the time all the preparations for his journey to Patna were completed, there was an understanding between John Deuchars and Julia Coatsworth. In jasmine-scented summerhouses such promises are often made.

Chapter Five

Helen watched the rain fall and picked up the small advertisement which her mother had cut out from a newspaper and brought back to the house. Sylvia, fresh from an encounter with an aggrieved tradesman, seized upon something to divert her. She held the paper to her forehead, weeping. That it had come to this! That she, Sylvia Jennings, should be forced to consider leaving her own home to go among strangers for paid work! Like all her other emotional storms, however, it passed. The paper was discarded.

May arrived, but spring was late and cold. In two days' time, Helen would be seventeen. She made a list of her difficulties. Her stuff skirts rubbed against her legs, her jacket was too small to fit around her bosom and her shoes were in no condition for travelling. She had reached a decision. Her mother had returned from the visit south with no news and still less money. She had been transported from the warmth and plenty of her aunt's to a damp and uncertain future. Life was impossible, her mother was bad tempered and tearful, and they were being refused credit everywhere. It was clear that something had to change. It was not her mother's fault that they were in such circumstances. Helen knew that to leave home would be difficult, her mother being left alone without her support. With each day the attentions of the landlord were becoming more difficult to manage. Her mother would not rebuff him firmly.

Helen had read and reread the advertisement.

A companion is required. This position requires a female person to attend a married lady and her children to join her husband in Calcutta, India.

Helen had decided to apply. She reasoned to herself, *I have no prospects and no money, and I cannot change that by staying here. Yet, I must leave my mother when I know that she needs me. I may need to go without a word and I may never find John. I have no money of my own to return.*

The first step had been the hardest, but it was now all settled. Helen thought with quiet satisfaction that it was the only way. She told her mother, and was subjected to tears and bitter words. She answered the advertisement and agreed to take up the position of travelling companion and mother's help within the month. Helen would join a Major's lady and her children in London before setting sail for India. She had always known that, as soon as she was old enough, she would leave and find her own way. It was just that this was a little earlier than planned and therefore more difficult than she had anticipated. It had also involved a little deceit. In the back of her mind as justification was the thought that she had a friend in India who needed her. She considered the family at Deerfield, who both she and her mother had decided not to involve. Eleanor was concerned for her niece, but she had found herself unable to offer Helen a home at the Parsonage with her precious daughters. She had acknowledged some relief when, on a cold January day, Helen returned north with her mother.

Helen was intuitive and knew when people wanted to be rid of her. Eleanor had not really been the same since John's departure. The house had been unnaturally quiet; not even gifts from Deerfield Hall had lifted the mood at the Parsonage. Helen had told one or two white lies to her mother and to her prospective employer, but who could blame her? To her mother she had said that the MacLennans were known to the family at Deerfield. She told her that she had written to Eleanor who had approved the arrangements. She had even gone on to say that the Major and her father had been in the same regiment, which was absolutely untrue. Sylvia said that she could not remember anyone of that name, but Helen observed that her mother had never had a good memory. Sylvia, weary of life, agreed and did not feel equal to contacting Eleanor to discuss the arrangements. She remembered the very difficult interview with her cousin about the management of young daughters.

Matters were settled. Helen told the Major's lady that she was eighteen. She said that her father was dead and that, although her mother had remarried, she felt unwelcome in the new household. She claimed to be of good family and gave vague details of her mothers connection with the Deerfield estate advising that she had a relative already in India which was true. She had been able to produce a very good character reference, not too fulsome in praise but not hiding her strengths. Helen signed it herself. Once Helen had begun to embelish, it was much easier than was comfortable. Always quick and resourceful, she told herself that this was another situation in which she must manage her own affairs. In no time, her part fabricated other life became real and preferable to her.

Helen had no French and she played the pianoforte very badly, but the Major's lady appeared to think she was qualified for the position on the strength of her reference. Helen felt she could manage the few requirements of the post in terms of looking after the children. They were very small, so most of the tasks would be related to their practical care rather than their education.

She could not have known that Major Callum MacLennan was careless of his little family. He had realised, in speaking to fellow officers before his departure for India, that he had not made very satisfactory arrangements. He was not wholeheartedly behind the plan for his family to follow him, so did not attempt to make amends. In any case, he was just about to sail, so they would have to shift for themselves. The army was encouraging more wives to travel to India and his would be one of the first to make the arduous journey, but the Major would have been happy if his wife had stayed behind.

When they met, Helen thought Mrs Claire MacLennan appeared rather frail. The two little girls were only four years and a few months old respectively. The baby, Hannah, was still at breast! She could not imagine India would suit the family at all.

Helen knew that Eleanor had received very few letters from John. She had no doubt he was busy taking care of the East India Company's interests. She was also sure she would find him. God forbid that John was ill, or worse. She had heard her father's officer friends joking that a white bride could name her price. She pushed the thought from her mind.

Helen and the little MacLennan family joined *The Duke of Grafton* at Deal. The small flotilla of cockboats hurled themselves at the waves, appearing to make no headway. These tiny boats were loaded down with all the essentials the passengers would need, including their cabin furniture.

They were late to board and, despite a promise of provision being made in the poop cabins, without male assistance they found that their accommodation had been reallocated. Helen protested, but to no avail. There were only five officers on duty and they were most unhelpful. Helen and the MacLennans were escorted by an officer in blue uniform with gilt buttons to their new accommodation, which did not improve their lot. They were as good as in steerage. All four of the little group were expected to inhabit a tiny space into which the smell of the bilges penetrated.

It was a risk to take an infant to sea, but Claire McLennan would not leave her children at home, despite her mother-in-law's protests. Hannah, a pale little thing, cried little for so young a child. On several occasions Helen returned from the cook with one or two additions to poor-quality meals in an attempt to entice Claire to eat. Although the little one suckled, she did so half-heartedly. She could not be tempted by the 'burgoo' oat mash which Helen prepared as a desperate substitute for Claire's milk. Esme, the older child, ate little but seemed to be the more resilient of the two girls. The Ship's Surgeon was an unfeeling man who, when asked to help said, 'Had

I known that the baby was still at the breast, I would have forbidden you a berth at all'.

This scolding was accompanied by improvement in neither their accommodation nor their fare, but two kindly passengers allowed them access to their own provisions. The passage was rough from the outset. Despite the ministrations of a fellow passenger, Hannah became weaker. Two older ladies in another part of the ship developed a fever and the passengers' instinct for self-preservation led to an unseemly scramble for provisions. Helen was furious to find that Claire had very limited resources with which to purchase the extras that would have made the voyage more bearable. She could not understand why the Major could have allowed his wife to travel with so little. It made no difference in the end; the younger child died within weeks of sailing.

Major MacLennan had embarked with his regiment in early April following a long-awaited promotion. It was clear from Claire's account that her husband was careless. However, she was a devoted wife and would not hear any criticism of him. Helen came to understand that it was unlikely that Major McLennan would be at the port to greet them. Nor could she find out that any arrangements been made to secure them accommodation or servants upon arrival.

Their only good fortune was that also travelling in a small, curtained-off area in steerage was a widow returning to India to resume her vocation. To date her work there had received little encouragement or support from the representatives of government but this had made her more determined and resourceful. Cholera is also determined, and had carried off Margaret Alexander's husband just as he had begun to make some small impact in Calcutta. His wife had not evaporated in the hot sun or succumbed to illness. It might have been said that, constitutionally, she was tougher than her husband. By contrast, his evangelising fire in partnership with the burning Indian heat, had slowly immolated him.

After his death the Glasgow Missionary Society acknowledged that Mrs Margaret Alexander had done as much good as her husband in spreading the Gospel and penetrating the closed societies of women. This had not stopped them recalling her home, much to her chagrin. They explained that her husband had been their nominated man. Although her medicine and her teaching experience had been useful, the society would not allow her to continue the work alone. They would sponsor another man who might take over. Margaret Alexander had nonetheless returned to India to begin again on her own. This time she would give equal attention to medicine and education, leaving evangelising to others. This is not to say she did not have great faith – she loved her Lord. Margaret Alexander was ready to work hard. Equipped with previous experience, significant local knowledge and a formidable reputation, she had embarked for India again alone. She had the advantage of independent means to ensure no interfering person in Glasgow would dictate terms to her.

Helen found that in many ways they were kindred spirits. Despite the age difference there was a practical meeting of minds. Helen could not fully understand Margaret's personal mission or why she would want to give up a comfortable life. Margaret explained about her sense of purpose, her faith and her calling. By the end of the long voyage they were firm friends. Helen doubted if she could have managed things with Claire after Hannah's death without Margaret's help. Margaret thought she had found a potential helper in her important work.

Margaret Alexander had a somewhat different approach to that of her late husband. Helen learned that he had been trained by disciples of Carey, the greatest of missionaries – the same Carey whose constitution and temperament had let him down at last. Mrs Alexander had surprised everyone, including herself, in adjusting to the climate and the demands of missionary life. She had been able to penetrate areas of Indian society which were closed to her husband. She loved the people. Recently she had been asked to provide medicines and medical services to the younger girls kept in the harem and to teach some English using amusing little storybooks. These women were in purdah, so every amusement was welcome, and they were very amused by Margaret Alexander's ugliness. In giving intensely uncomfortable women basic medical care and spending time with them, she was able to use her medicine chest in tandem with reading books. At first she was thought to be no threat, and the officials in the palace even hung around her asking her questions about the English. She felt herself to be in no danger.

Her appearance was deceptive. She was small, her brown hair piled high into a thick, tight bun. Her skin was freckled, the effect of exposure to the sun. Her grey eyes were lively and she had a long nose, a wide mouth and not an ounce of spare flesh upon her. She had no appreciable bosom. Margaret had never been beautiful but Robert Alexander had not married her for her looks. He had found her to be a good Christian, a practical woman, and saw her as an intelligent helpmeet in his mission. She had, she told Helen, been disappointed in foolish love early, but confided that she would have made a boy soldier a very unsatisfactory wife. She had loved her Robert and had been fiercely protective of him, although he was not a demonstrative husband. She would have liked to have his child but they had not been fortunate and she would not marry again.

All these things Helen gleaned as the ship lay motionless on what seemed like a sheet of glass. There was not a breath of wind and, on Margaret's advice; Claire and Helen lay shaded to all possible extent from the burning sun as the ship cracked in the heat. They listened as Margaret talked quietly and comfortingly. The hot air so dried Helen's throat that she could barely speak. Claire lay in her cot. In the cooler evenings Margaret spoke of the intense man who had convinced her that she should share his life of hardship. She told of his refusal to use any of her money and his reassurance that the fact she was older was an advantage. He had told her that a younger woman might not cope with the rigours of the life and the demands of the work. She spoke of his fervour, but not of his love.

Helen sensed a sadness that in her younger life Margaret had not felt she had been loved. A sense of obligation and duty were, Helen felt, poor substitutes. Helen intended to have a man feel passionately for her or not at all. Margaret described the support her parents had given once they realised that God demanded she should do His work in India. She told of her husband's ill health and how he had refused to go home to a safer position. They had been told this was his only hope. She told of watching the ship that would have taken them to safety sail out of the Hooghly River; of deciding never to regret again because it was too painful. Before his death, Robert Alexander had urged her to keep his mission open and, if brought home, to use her money to maintain it in absentia. He made her promise to return herself or find a protégé who would carry on his work.

Helen could not help but feel that he must have been a demanding man to stipulate so much. Before these thoughts had fully formed, however, Margaret Alexander read them.

'My father never forgave him, I think, for putting my life so much at hazard. I never saw my father alive after I married and left for India. I suppose they felt they had lost both children. My brother was killed in '16, a major in a Sepoy regiment. After he died my parents only had me and then I too left for India. They felt we had deserted them, I suppose, but I have no regrets. My father remembered me in his will and when I returned home I found that I am more than comfortable. I have been able to revive my establishment in Calcutta and I feel renewed and ready to continue. It will not be exactly as Robert would have wished, but I will not neglect the Lord in the things I mean to do. It is unfortunate that I have been unable to persuade another to come to help me. There was one who, after my talks at home in Glasgow, might have joined me. I would not take him as a husband and he would not come any other way. It was not to be. Do not be hard on my husband. I return because it is what I want. I did not leave India out of choice. Now I return on my own terms.'

Helen felt very comfortable in talking with this softly spoken woman. She told Mrs Alexander of her own difficult days when her mother and she had barely managed; of the help they had received from Colonel Roberts. This help, she felt, would have been enough if her mother had been careful, but she was not. Her mother had always felt that, having been brought up as a lady, certain things were due to her. Margaret asked of Helen's father. She spoke quietly of his intermittent presence in the home as she grew up; of the parties when his officer friends would come to visit and how she was required to amuse them. She spoke of her father's use of alcohol and his very hard hand. Helen had seen her mother beaten and was determined that no man should have such power over her. She told Margaret Alexander that she was glad when her father left, however straitened their circumstances. Helen even told her that she had, in despair, stolen.

Margaret had suspected that this flight to India was a desperate act for one so young. She was not demonstrative and simply took Helen's hand in hers in a silent promise of friendship. Helen wondered aloud if they would ever reach land. It was rumoured that storms lay ahead of this deathly quiet. She had heard from the other passengers of the fate of the *Grosvenor*. Margaret shuddered.

'Helen, dear, please do not mention the *Grosvenor*,' she whispered. 'Who would ever forget that ship, or her desperate passengers and crew?'

Fate was not tempted, and the *Duke of Grafton* reached the City of Palaces safely on 30th September 1829. By the time the family reached Calcutta, Claire was ill. Tightly clutching her remaining little girl, she was carried off the ship, unable to walk. Helen and her charges were offered rooms in the very small house belonging to Margaret, just until the Major came to collect his wife and child. It was agreed that Margaret would occupy the ground floor of the low, whitewashed house behind the court. The little family would be installed on the floor above. A supply of saltpetre was secured to be dissolved in bowls of water, a process which greatly reduced the temperature of the water, cooling vessels placed in it and the immediate surroundings. Several servants were engaged. It was only then that the Major's lady, like a wilting rose placed in cooler and gentler conditions, began to revive.

Helen realised that the servants were common to both households and this encouraged the intimacy that grew between them. She felt that, all things considered, their situation could be a great deal worse. Then the south-east monsoon arrived, late and devastating. It washed life and willpower away. Vegetables, fruit and people were carried around head-high to keep them out of the mud. The bedding smelt of cheese and the air hung around the little house like a mouldy curtain.

Chapter Six

John sat crouched in a small boat, having given up wiping his soaking face. They were making slow progress up river. It had rained hard all morning, fast-flowing streams cascaded at each side of the main channel. The water washed down the crumbling banks, carrying vegetation into the river. The crew were fully engaged in maintaining progress, fending off the larger branches that threatened to hole the barge. It felt as if the earth was dissolving in the deluge. John was now fully briefed regarding profit and the poppy and he appreciated how he was expected to serve the interests of the Company, but enthusiasm was difficult to sustain in torrential rain. He reflected on the events of previous weeks.

During conversations in his hothouse, Sir Josiah Coatsworth had explained many things. Apparently, in the absence of silver – which was far too scarce a commodity to pour into China in exchange for tea and silk – the company had found a very lucrative substitute. The Home Secretary said that opium was something that the Chinese wanted as much as silver; they could not do without it. It was a commodity which the Company could supply for a modest outlay in comparison to the returns. He explained the complexities of the trade; it was, he said, 'a question of economic necessity'.

The Abolitionists, though supported by all rational men, had not yet set the slaves free. There were still large subsidies on slave-produced goods in the Americas. Those subsidies were very precious to the occupants of country seats back in England. Members of Parliament protected their masters' interests with tenacity, so the Company did all it could to maintain profit in a competitive market.

'Our imperative,' Sir Josiah had said, 'is to keep the wheels of trade turning in India until the slave is free. Indian labour is so efficient and so attractively cheap that we do not have to keep slaves. Nonetheless, we look to the day the Americas compete with us on level ground. For the moment, we gain not only the pecuniary but also the moral dividend and we do this with the aid of that most valuable commodity – the opium poppy.'

Coatsworth was passionate about India. 'The Indian is industrious, naturally so. He will work until he drops – it is part of his religion, his pride. Africans will not work for the plantation owners as free men. They know that when they are freed – for that day will come – they will not be able to compete economically with us here.'

Hugh Mowbray saluted Sir Josiah's knowledge of economics. He was very determined to have his silk waistcoats and emphatic that the King should have his tea.

'Sir Josiah is such a sensible man,' Mowbray told John. 'He knows that if we were rid of the subsidies on West African trade India could come into her own. Until then we need to use what resources we have – and that includes the poppy.'

It was already mid-September, late in the season to travel north. Mr Mowbray made several pointed comments about how fortunate John was in having attracted the notice of Sir Josiah Coatsworth, and that he had not minded at all doing without him so that he could visit his sweetheart. He had been able to organise their departure single-handedly without John's help, as it pleased Sir Josiah to trust him. He would expect John to make up the time lost once they reached Patna. John received much advice and many commissions regarding the collection of plant specimens for Sir Josiah. Mr Mowbray told John that, 'As much as I would wish Sir Josiah to have his plants and his drawings, I hope that this plant mania will not interfere with your other duties'.

Coatsworth had particularly liked to talk to John of his home, wistfully remarking that John's description of family life at Deerfield reminded him of his own early years in Cheshire. They had discussed the Reverend Deuchars' opinion upon enclosure and the effects of industry on the land. Sir Josiah confided in John that, once the Company could spare him, he would wish to return home. He had cautioned against the risks involved in encouraging new industry, reflecting that speculation had been the cause of many a family's ruin. He remarked to John that he, of all people, knew this to be true.

Sir Josiah never remained morose for long and John recalled this as the Home Secretary recommended the pursuit of the floral arts above all others. As a gentleman's son, he felt John would understand. This resulted in John copying rare blooms, and his drawings were much admired. John remembered the sweet smell of the hothouse, his darling's hair mingling with the fragrance of jasmine in the heat of the afternoon. He pictured Julia's face as he had taken his leave of her. He would show them all. He would bring in the poppy harvest, build a reputation in the Company, and afterwards Julia would be his. He remembered with a mixture of joy and fear their last meeting – so many things he felt he wanted to say before leaving. John pictured her lovely face framed by the flower-laden arches of the large doors to the garden. He remembered how he had held and kissed the hands of his beautiful Julia. Safe and dry in his breast pocket nestled a curl of her golden hair which he had wrapped in a portion of neatly hemmed handkerchief. Beside it was a sprig of jasmine.

Chapter Seven

I n the heat of an October afternoon, tea was being served in the makeshift parlour of the little house off Court House Lane. From the upper chamber, Helen had a fine view of the church. She could just see a glint of the Hooghly River beyond Fort William's stables and the saltpetre godowns. There was hardly a breath of air. It was the middle of the afternoon and the room was quiet, the weather unseasonably hot. Although everyone had been so pleased when the Major came, his visit was short and he left without making any proper arrangements for his family. His wife was still frail from the voyage, Margaret Alexander had plainly said she was not making good enough progress.

Claire never complained but, despite the relief at being on dry land and the joy at seeing her husband, she did not improve. She suffered from an intermittent fever and could not keep food down. Margaret prepared a strong Chirata mixture from the gentian herb. Helen sat by Claire's bed holding the dish to her lips. She felt helpless and angry that Claire should suffer. Surely somebody could have prevented her following her heartless husband halfway round the world. He appeared indifferent to Claire and his little daughter, Esme. He had made it clear that as Claire was unable to prepare a home for him she would hardly require his money above the room rent he proposed to give Margaret Alexander. He had not spoken of payment for Helen's services to the little family.

Margaret had found it necessary to point out to him that Helen was owed her salary from disembarkation and that money for food would be required. She was clear that her own household could not feed everyone without his support. Helen had spent the morning fuming on this as she tended Claire. Helen tried to get her to sip the bitter medicine from a spoon but it just ran down her neck in rivulets, staining her white gown. Claire cried softly, like a child, for her husband but Major MacLennan did not return. The child, Esme, was now given over to one of Margaret's young servants, the great-niece of her rock and right hand, Badshah Raj, now retired from his Sepoy regiment. He was devoted to Margaret Alexander, as he had been to her brother with whom he had served. These new arrangements had been made when it became clear that Helen would have to take over complete care of Claire. To make matters worse, they had run out of saltpetre and the little house was like an oven.

Claire had become painfully thin, lying in only her nightclothes. Her hair stuck to her forehead. Margaret had said there was a real chance she would not live, and yet she hung on. She tossed in her bed until she was soaked. In the long hours of the hot afternoon, Helen considered her options and decided that, if Claire did not survive, the remaining child should return to England. She knew she herself would be pressed to take it, but she would not go. She had not accomplished what she had set out to do, trapped in the sickroom. She must tell Margaret that she needed to find John.

Margaret made her night-time visit to inspect the patient. Helen was in the little space created by a thin curtain adjacent to Claire's bed. Margaret knew how confined Helen had been and that she needed a change of air, but Claire could not be left alone. That evening Margaret stayed longer than usual. She felt that Claire, who was sleeping quietly, appeared to be a little better. Helen, emerging from behind the muslin screen, looked pale. Margaret paused at the door and before leaving asked Helen if she would like to accompany her on a visit to Government House late the following evening. They could arrange for someone to watch over Claire. Margaret explained that it was in relation to her work among the Mahratta's household. She said she did not relish going alone and would value Helen's support. Margaret confided that she had treated a female member of the Mahratta's family after she was delivered of an unwanted baby girl. This had been against the express wish of the husband's mother. To compound the issue, the mother and her infant had lived. The displeasure of the royal family had been made known to His Excellency Sir Alfred Venables, the Governor-General.

Margaret had already received a visit from one of the Governor-General's minions, who firmly advised that in future she must not concern herself in the delicate matters of the Mahratta's household. Mr Chaudhuri had been business-like.

'Will you give me your word, madam, that you will desist from involving yourself in the lives of the women of the harem? They are cared for by their own people in time-honoured fashion. Given the importance of other negotiations, it is the first rule of the Company that we should not interfere. It is our very first and most important rule.'

He made no headway. Margaret, irritated at his apparent indifference to the conditions in which these women lived, was equally indifferent to Company rules.

She told Helen that she had said to Mr Chaudhuri that she was not governed by the Company rules and would take her medicines and books wherever she chose. She would not refuse help of either medical or spiritual kind, no matter how important other matters might be to the Council, especially when the alternatives were cowdung poultices and ignorance.

'I fail to see,' Margaret said to Helen in an angry whisper so that she did not disturb Claire, 'how my small efforts have anything to do with the Governor-General. If you could see these young girls, some are no more than fourteen. One is from the far north, I think, a gift to the Mahratta. Helen, her husband is fifty at least and had her privies stuffed with apricots for his pleasure. I am sorry, I know you are young, but I think you have seen much to know about such men. I treated her, that is all. The bites he inflicted were infected and no other would touch them. This, mark you, is a girl carrying a child past the time when she should have been left alone. He evidently had to have her as his absolute favourite. They are all so very young and can expect no help from the older wives. The older women are made very jealous by the attention these younger girls receive. It was not like this before the Company came. The people the Company has favoured are the worst kind. The good old families are left to live in near poverty, robbed of their rightful lands.'

Helen had no idea of the history of such arrangements, but she listened as Margaret continued.

'The mother-in-law in this case thought this young girl had her son under a spell and wanted her dead. I delivered the child but I had no idea until recently that it had survived. It was a girl, you see, and they did not want her.' Margaret noticed that Helen had said nothing and was much paler. 'I apologise, my dear. Such a tirade, you are tired and I forget myself. You are young and new to India. I really do most sincerely apologise. This conversation is unsuitable for you – forgive me.'

Helen paused before speaking quietly.

'You know I have not had a conventional childhood. I confess I am taken aback because you have said these girls are younger than me with children of their own and, worse, old husbands. The circumstances you have described only fill me with a greater admiration for you. I am glad to be made aware. I need to learn so much, as quickly as possible, if I am to help you in this work. In a sense, although it sounds shocking, I feel the Major's lady is in a somewhat similar position, except for the apricots. She is so young and defenceless, and he is such an unfeeling husband.'

Helen turned and looked at Claire's sleeping form.

'I have not left this room for days,' she went on. 'A change of air would do me good. If I can support you at this meeting with the authorities it is the least I can do after all you have done to help me.'

Margaret smiled and was grateful. She had received a summons to attend on the Home Secretary and knew him to be formidable. There was no negotiation – the letter stipulated time and place and advised her to be punctual. So it was that Helen, having made everything secure at home, accompanied Margaret to face Sir Josiah Coatsworth.

Sir Josiah did not keep them waiting. Helen had taken great care with her toilette. Margaret had made no special effort at all but clutched her Bible and her medicine box. She came ready to explain the contents of one and hoped she would not need to spell out the meaning of the other. She had prepared a pithy speech about the conditions in which young girls of the harem lived, bearing children to men when not yet grown themselves. She was ready to outline the vices she had encountered, which she felt were the direct consequences of age-old tradition. She intended to make Sir Josiah squirm with embarrassment.

Margaret had described these arrangements to Helen as 'the captivity of child women by immoral persons'. She meant to use this particular phrase with Coatsworth and she set her jaw as she stepped into the magnificent hallway of his home.

'Helen, observe this gaudy and sinful ostentation,' said Margaret, too loudly for Helen's comfort. 'This could be ancient Rome.' She raised her head, addressing the ornate plasterwork. 'Oh, teach me thy way, oh Lord, and lead me in a plain path because of mine enemies.'

They were shown into a high-ceilinged room, white flowering jasmine cascading across the ceiling and down the walls, filling it with fragrance. This led into a cool chamber in which there stood a large desk covered with papers. Sweet smells wafted through a low doorway and made Helen feel hungry. The walls of the room were hung with silver-and-red embroidered silk depicting hunting scenes, castles and fast-flowing rivers.

Against a back wall stood some very ornate chairs. The large window openings were shaded with blinds. Helen could not help but notice the hanging candelabra laden with candles and wondered what such a monstrosity would cost. Smiling china putti frolicked among the fruit bowls on a magnificently carved buffet table. It was a very ornate room for an office. Margaret's brow had creased into a frown. Helen thought, correctly as it happened, that her companion would be wondering how much work was actually done in here. A tall man, his long, shapely legs elegantly crossed, sat slightly aside from the desk, whence he had an excellent view of their arrival.

'Ladies,' he purred. 'How delightful to see you. Will you have some tea?'

He clicked his fingers and presently a servant appeared with refreshments, disappearing as quietly as she had come. She exchanged a glance with Helen – did she smile? Helen could not be sure.

While contemplating her surroundings, Helen noticed that she was being observed by a pair of very dark eyes, shining from under eyebrows that wound upwards in curls towards a high forehead. The gentleman's cheeks were covered in impressive sideburns and he had a particularly fine moustache. The backs of his hands were also covered with dark, silk-like hairs. He was, or rather had been, quite handsome. Helen thought upon this and could see by the way he looked at her that he was equally aware that she was young and pretty. Instead of immediately hounding Margaret, as she had expected, he would know who Helen was and whence her family came. He smiled at her – a charming smile, she thought, for such an elderly man. Surprisingly, Helen found herself telling him that her father had worn the sash; he had been in His Majesty's Light Infantry and had seen action against the Gurkhas in '16. She explained her situation to him and emphasised Margaret's great kindness towards her.

Helen told Sir Josiah more than she intended and was sorry to see that this had made Margaret cross. She consoled herself that she had managed to omit that she did not currently know the whereabouts of her father, but felt she had gone so far that she might as well enquire about John. She mentioned that she had a cousin in India who was not in uniform, and gave his name. Helen was pleased to hear that John was known to Sir Josiah, and further that the latter had spoken with him often before he had gone north to Patna.

'They are expected back sometime in late February,' said Sir Josiah, vaguely.

He added that his daughter, Julia, would be pleased to welcome him on his return, which rather took Helen aback.

Margaret felt that it was time to get on with the matter at hand. She had heard quite enough of family histories and asked Coatsworth stiffly, 'Do you have particular enquiries to make of me? I have a very busy day tomorrow and Miss Helen is needed at home.'

Sir Josiah turned slowly and formally to Margaret and, after making polite enquiries as to her health, came to the point.

'Madam, my representative has, I think, spoken to you and I can but try to put to you again the delicate matter of the Mahratta's family. Perhaps I can do this with a little more clarity than he has already done. I know it is quite pointless to talk to you about our policy of non-interference in local custom and practice at any level, whether in the street or in a princely palace. You appear to feel you have a mandate to usurp their very religion; you are unlikely to be swayed by persuasion as to non-interference in custom and practice. I see it is of no matter to you that they are underpinned by centuries of culture and tradition.'

Helen heard this and wondered how it was possible to be so insulting yet sound so completely charming. Sir Josiah placed his long fingers together in front of his face, his elbows resting on the table, and stroked his luxurious moustaches.

'I put it to you instead that, if we have a young, impressionable prince, then who better to guide and educate him than ourselves? We civilise him, we prevent him learning from his devious and unprincipled uncles. We protect him from the complexities of early decision-making and we guide him to adulthood. This process shapes his views and forms over time a most important allegiance.

We may require him at a future date, for example, to discipline his neighbour or his uncles, in which action we will of course assist him. I am sure that you see the importance of maintaining harmony with the prince and his family. It is, madam, more important than the life of one of the many young women in that place or, indeed, the life of an infant. There is, as you know, a spectacular abundance of both commodities in this country.'

Helen did not see the man breathe during this quiet address. Before Margaret could protest he held up his hand, rather as a spider would raise one leg.

'To conclude, we must leave the running of his household entirely to him. He must still feel and live like a prince. He must be in control of his princely life. We cannot afford to upset him – it is a matter of his honour, and family honour is everything. Once he is upset, he begins to question our very special relationship. Am I making myself clear to you? I strongly suggest that we must not interfere within the confines of his household. We must leave the administration of it entirely up to him, to act and do as he sees fit.'

'Sir Josiah,' Margaret answered very deliberately, 'I well know the extent of your Company's interference in the affairs of India. I think in terms of interference my small works are insignificant by comparison. I am dependent upon your goodwill, because if you chose to you could see to it that I was sent home on the next ship. You must know that the living conditions of these women are intolerable, and if you could only see –'

She was not allowed to finish. Coatsworth raised that hand of his as if shielding his face from a bright sun.

'Madam,' he said very quietly, 'I do not wish to see anything other than the maintenance of proper order and the successful organisation of business. In effect, the progress of India towards her true destiny as the trading hub of the world.' He leant forward, continuing gently but firmly, 'I have personal experience of the passion of the disciples of the old Serampore Brotherhood and you are hewn from the same tree. Could you find it in yourself, madam, to help me, and I will then help you?

'I am anxious to see the conditions in which people live here improved, naturally. This can be achieved by improving India through careful and consistent administration. It is years since we experienced serious unrest, but we have not forgotten Vellore and I would not suggest an Indian change his clothes, never mind the tradition of centuries, if I thought it would affect our trade. Trade, madam, is all. Do you need supplies, more suitable rooming, perhaps some monetary aid? Is there anything I can arrange for you which might help us reach an accommodation?'

Margaret felt very alone – Coatsworth was a powerful orator. She looked at him with her wise grey eyes.

'You have forgotten, Sir Josiah, that I am concerned with truth and faith. Your earthly business and pursuit of riches is as nothing to me. Remember here we have no continuing city – you cannot take your jewels into the next life. I thank you for your advice and for your kind offers of help, but we will not agree. I am committed to assisting the sick and the poor in any way I can. I teach a little and I do read from the scriptures, which surely you must not object to. I have no need of an earthly guide, in fact there is nothing I need from you. Please leave me to decide on the course of action most appropriate to my mission. I cannot promise you that I will ignore the plight of these women. You should know that I will continue to give them aid. After all, it is your wilful promotion of these puppet princes which has destroyed the natural civilised order of this place.'

Coatsworth was stung; he prided himself on his persuasive powers. Margaret Alexander, he thought, looked ugly. In his experience this appeared to be a prerequisite for the missionary vocation. Yet she had a power about her, the poor misguided woman. He could see her knuckles fastened white against her Bible. Such conviction and determination he had to admire, however inconvenient.

Helen looked from one to the other in what seemed a very long silence. They would never agree, both so convinced of their respective purpose. She tried to measure the weight of each argument and failed. Helen knew Margaret's worth, but she also felt this man's authority, knowledge and the power of his personality. The effect upon her was not unpleasant.

The tension in the room was broken by the arrival of more tea, which was taken without much conversation on Margaret's part. Sir Josiah talked away as if there had been no disagreement at all. Helen thought that this must be the diplomat in him; he was quite a wit.

As they were about to take their leave, Coatsworth spoke as if in afterthought.

'I wonder, would you like to attend a small gathering in honour of a visiting prince? He is quite our most magnificent yet, and we get on famously. He is interested in improvements in agriculture – you might approve of him.' Looking closely at Margaret, he added in a lower voice, 'He has most civilised arrangements within his own quarters. It is only bearable to gather in the cooler weather, you know. There is someone else who will be with us who I would very much like this young person to meet.'

He was now observing Helen, who was in the process of inspecting a large orchid. Sir Josiah thought it would look very lovely in her hair.

'Mrs Alexander, it would please me if you would bring with you your delightful young friend. I understand she and my daughter have shared interests. There are also some influential members of Calcutta society who may be of assistance to you in your less controversial work, for I know you are in need of medicines, whatever you say.'

Margaret, astonished at the gall of the man, looked from their host to Helen. He was impossible, but she had heard the Raja was a wise man and he might be useful to her. Self-interest succeeded where Coatsworth's powers of persuasion had not. Margaret agreed to attend. There were, she thought, sponsors in the unlikeliest of places – even in Company circles. Nevertheless, on her return home and after reflection, she could not understand why she had not managed Sir Josiah better, and was cross with herself for the remainder of the day.

Chapter Eight

Helen had never seen so much light and splendour as they approached the mansion on the following evening for the reception. In fact, it was astonishing to her that there could be so much light at night and out of doors. The grounds were lit by a thousand torches from the gateway all the way up to the house, sending orange sparks high into the night sky. There were lights in every window so that the mansion looked as if it were on fire against the blackness beyond. The only other light was the moon. It sat over the sea as if competing with this earthly magnificence. The doors to the mansion were open wide. At either side stood three enormous sepoys dressed in white with red turbans topped with coiled silver-and-black serpents.

Inside was all gold and deepest red, crowds of people thronging in long silk gowns. Huge plates of delicacies and sweetmeats were carried at head height. From the gaping mouths of silver elephants attendants poured a fragrant liquid into crystal cups. An orchestra played and guests clamoured. Helen felt it astonishing that Mr Handel was being played so very far from an English assembly room. It all looked and sounded wonderful.

'Has everything that is valuable and fine been transported to this one place for the evening?' Helen whispered to Margaret.

'No, dear,' Margaret replied with a smile. 'All the palaces have their own finery. India has more wealth of this kind than you can imagine, and it belongs to the most unlikely and undeserving of people.'

They had moved along the hallway and through some enormous teak doors, at either side of which ornamental table-pieces rose, almost reaching the glowing chandeliers. Large tables were laden with cascades of fruit. The ballroom was hung with silk canopies. People moved like a shining wave across the dance floor. Helen could hear the voice of Sir Josiah Coatsworth above the noise, inviting his guests to come through towards the supper tables. Entertainments were underway at the far end of the room; conjurers and jugglers appeared, making their way among the crowd who clapped and laughed at their skill.

Helen and Margaret had arrived very late, as Margaret had not returned from her work until long after dark. She had said she was really too tired to attend, but felt that she could not disappoint her friend by refusing to go. Margaret Alexander had not always been immune to the charms of an evening party. Grown older and wiser, she was reluctant to have anything to do with such vanity. She was, however, drawn by the promise of the assistance to which Sir Josiah had alluded, and felt she could not overlook a chance to discuss her work with potential supporters.

It was an enormous gathering, but through the crush Coatsworth saw Helen and came to her. It was kind that he did not comment on the gown borrowed from the Major's wife. It was very plain and had been let out at the bosom. Helen had, with assistance, attached a border of lace at the hem to lengthen it and had sewn a silk scarf from her portmanteau below the bosom which tied at the back. She wore it with blue kid gloves that did not match. It would have to do. She remembered the scarf's beautiful owner with some shame, as she had never returned the item; but Helen saw no purpose in dwelling on such thoughts. She had made up her own hair. It was plainly done and reliant upon her natural curls, she had to be content with the result.

She stepped sideways to avoid a juggler and found herself facing a magnificent robed personage. The tassels on the sleeves of his scarlet *aba* shimmered. The long coat fell in silken folds to the ground. Fastened around his waist was a fabulous, jewel-encrusted belt.

Helen noted that the sleeves of his coat were lined in bright-green silk. His hands were covered in gold rings set with precious stones. Helen could not see his fingers. He was tall and wonderful to look at. She was sure this must be a Raja, and she put out her hand in greeting; the magnificent personage was immediately closely surrounded by attendants. Helen was startled for a moment, then Sir Josiah Coatsworth glided through the gap and the attendants melted into the background. Sir Josiah slid her arm through his, pulling her firmly into a curtsey as he bowed low.

'Your Highness, we are most honoured,' he purred. 'May I present Mrs Margaret Alexander and Miss Helen Jennings, recently arrived in Calcutta? Ladies, His Highness the Maharaja of Patna.'

Even Margaret had to admit that Sir Josiah looked splendid, with his moustaches waxed and his hair and eyebrows tamed. He was dressed in tight-fitting black hose and a short red ornamented jacket. His waistcoat was a marvellously coloured blood red and interwoven with gold and pink silk threads. His cravat was snow-white. He turned and spoke to an attendant, who went immediately to attend to the Maharaja's party. Then Sir Josiah turned to Helen.

'My dear young lady, I am so pleased you could come. Do you like what you see? Have you been attended to? Indeed, how you could not like what you see, for the young adore a party, do they not? Have you had some refreshments and are you going to view our entertainment?' Before she could respond, he continued, 'I have a further treat for you, as I promised. I always keep my promises, especially to young ladies.'

As he spoke, the attendant returned, accompanied by a man dressed in uniform. He had very fine sideburns.

For an instant, Helen's mind flew to a small, cold, whitewashed house in Newcastle. She looked at the figure that had appeared at

Sir Josiah's left shoulder and for Helen the room became suddenly silent. The mouths of those around her were moving but she could only stare at the stranger by Sir Josiah's side. Coatsworth thrust the man forward deliberately and, to the fellow's obvious annoyance, said, 'Jennings, you know this young person, I believe?'

Helen looked at Sir Josiah and then, finding her voice, stammered, 'Father! But I don't understand, how ... you come here. I thought – that is, we were told –'

It was fortunate that Margaret was close behind to catch her arm. Sir Josiah was speaking to her now.

'Do you not like my little surprise?' Coatsworth was delighted by it and continued, 'Your father is with us now, with the Company, you know. Oh, I see you did not know! Oh well, I expect you will have such news for each other. I will leave you together.'

Sir Josiah whirled off, his bounding energy determined to ensure his guests received everything it was within his gift to provide. He did so love arranging pleasant surprises – introducing Helen to her father and Margaret to Sir Alfred Venables, the Governor-General. Making arrangements and introductions was his particular talent.

Margaret had not met the Governor-General when she was last in India, but he appeared to have heard of her. Even she bowed very low to Sir Alfred. He was responsible for the Company's affairs in Bengal Presidency. She did not waste much time in pleasantries and went to work, as the Glasgow Missionary Society would have expected her to do. Sir Alfred was advised of the pressing and urgent need for more of her kind, and the immediate need for the authorities to take an interest in the health and education of the people of Bengal and increased official support for her work.

Sir Alfred Venables was a careful and courteous man. He listened politely to Margaret but was sceptical. He was interested in anything which would enhance both his and the Company's reputation and which would keep an interfering Leadenhall Street at bay. He was as God-fearing as the next man, but he vehemently disagreed with Margaret Alexander's approach. He did not believe in interfering in Indian affairs of religion, health or culture, unless the needs of business or a troublesome Maharaja made it impossible to do otherwise. He had learned a hard lesson some twenty years before and was now wholly occupied with judicial reforms of his own. As for the education of local women, good Lord, was she raving mad? Sir Alfred felt that there were some limited exceptions regarding interference, related to the practices of *suttee* and *thuggee*, which, he felt, any right-minded person would want to suppress.

'By God,' he told Margaret, 'I will do it.'

Religion was quite another matter, however, and much better left alone.

'I have read the work of Abbé Jean Antoine Dubois,' he advised Margaret, 'and I agree it has some merit. His knowledge of and immersion in all things culturally Indian is unsurpassed. I have attempted to urge others to take note, but you must know that in London these things appear very differently. We do what we can. We are very aware of our responsibilities to these people but we must be practical, politic and, above all, realistic. We will not achieve a little England here overnight.'

After a very animated discussion, Sir Alfred was wholly convinced that India did not need more of Margaret Alexander's kind. He wondered if he should order one of his staff to write to the Glasgow Missionary Society to advise them of just that. He instantly realised that if he did they would send another like her, and probably worse. He was diplomatically borne off by his assistant, to whom he exclaimed, 'Damn it, that Alexander woman has all but spoiled my evening. I am for home!' Sadly, this comment was repeated in the supper room, because Calcutta society is always in need of amusement.

Sir Josiah Coatsworth, oblivious to the Governor-General's discomfort, was delighted with himself, with the evening, with the magnificence of his house and with his guests. He extracted a huge amount of pleasure from placing this person here and that person there. He knew that he had a talent for juxtaposing people. He believed there was little which could not be achieved by careful arrangement coupled with charm and willpower. Time was not plentiful, aside from the rigours of the climate on the human constitution, even a strong one such as his. Change was afoot in the organisation of the Company. The old order was slipping away and there had lately been much more governmental interference. Yet a man still had to prosper, and he was determined that he would not go home without his share.

Sir Josiah's surprise introduction had left father and daughter staring at each other until Helen recovered and, in a torrent of words, managed to ask what in the devil he was doing in India and why he had not written to her mother. Her raised voice could be heard by those immediately around her, which was excruciating for Daniel Jennings. Helen shook with rage.

'My mother has hunted for you in Portsmouth and London. She could find out nothing but debt. She has been pursued throughout by furious tradesmen. We thought you bought out – no trace or word from you, no letter, nothing. Do you realise that Mother is still living in the same cold, damp house with the landlord who used to threaten you? We had no money, and had to live on the charity of others – and sometimes not even that. Your regiment has disowned you – your name is never spoken. Did you never mean to send us money, or see us again? The only things we were left with were your dreadful reputation and your debts.'

Daniel Jennings was now moving away, as Helen could be heard even above the noise of the assembly. Discomfiture was not a new sensation but he had not experienced it recently. In fact, he had made every attempt since his arrival to construct a respectable reputation and it was in danger because of this girl. He cursed Sir Josiah under his breath for placing him in such a ridiculous position, and in public. He did not enjoy being reminded that he had a wife, which he had neglected to mention, and now he would have to explain the appearance of a daughter.

Jennings was aware that he needed to quieten Helen. He said that of course he had not meant to disappear, but he had not wished to disgrace them with so many creditors pressing him. He had decided he would make his fortune and return with riches for her and for her mother. Helen did not believe him.

He said he was surprised but delighted to see her and seemed astonished that she had taken such a brave step herself. Before the evening was out he had made her promise not to speak to anyone about their circumstances until he could give her his full account in private. He said he would arrange for her to come to him at his house in the town, which, after some persuasion, she agreed to do. She was curious about his life and recent history but did not suppose the invitation would be honoured. All his other promises had failed to materialise, and this would be no different.

The evening of pleasure in Sir Josiah Coatsworth's magnificent house so eagerly anticipated had been dreadful. It had promised so much, but then the host had produced her father. To make matters worse, this was followed by a girl with luxurious blonde hair and the most wonderful dress Helen had ever seen telling her about an acquaintance with John Deuchars. She spoke of their 'special understanding' and, when pressed, would not say more. Helen could have wept with frustration. Afterwards she was aware she had been rude to Julia Coatsworth, hastily making her excuses and leaving. Helen was glad when Sir Josiah's mansion doors were closed behind her.

Julia had left Helen in no doubt of her feelings for John. Helen hoped she would be forgiven for the dreadful things she had said about John's family being so short of money that John had needed to come out to make his fortune to support them. Julia seemed to have been unmoved. She said quietly that she was aware how difficult things were in post-war Europe for the very best of families; that she had no doubt John's ability would bring him and his family good fortune. She had gone on endlessly about John's drawing, the hateful girl.

Then there was the appearance of her father – liar, debtor, and possibly worse. She knew he was as horrified to see her. Helen imagined he would do as little as he could to acknowledge her presence publicly and invite further awkward questions. She felt she needed Margaret's counsel. What should she write to her mother? Could he be persuaded to send any money home? It was frustrating and unfair; some things so eagerly anticipated often disappoint. Why was everything such a struggle for her when Julia Coatsworth had everything she could possibly want? Well, she could not have John – he belonged to *her*.

The only pleasant interludes had been the splendour of the place and that very exiting waltz, when Sir Josiah – who proved to be a capable and energetic dancer – spun her around the dance floor in a firm but expert grip. Helen thought that he must be very wealthy indeed.

As they made their way home in their palanquin, Helen did not hear Margaret's outraged description of her discussion with the Governor-General.

'To imagine,' said Margaret, 'that it is practicable to introduce a British court system in a land where people were dying of disease and ignorance. It was ridiculous!'

Margaret was explaining to Helen that, in her opinion, the Indian had access to perfectly serviceable laws in their own language and that the Governor-General was deluded in attempting to construct a Little England. Speaking as a Scot, she found that idea repulsive. When she eventually looked at Helen, she realised with annoyance that she was not listening. Margaret placed her hands on her lap and looked out into the night. It had been a waste of time, as she had thought it would. She shuddered as she recalled the ostentation. The only consolation was that at least Helen had enjoyed herself.

It was almost four days later that Claire died. The Major was not present. Helen held Claire's hand and promised to look after her child. At the end, Claire had forgotten the death of her younger daughter. Helen closed Claire's eyes and folded her hands across her tiny frame. She felt absolute relief. Helen allowed the servants to lay her out, while she took her tearful little girl downstairs to Margaret. She was furious at Claire's weakness. In Helen's eyes she had blindly followed her husband to India, idolised him, asked for him to the end, and died abandoned by him.

Claire had been distraught if ever Helen had made a critical remark – and for what? There had been no love, no acknowledgement from the Major, and now she was gone. There was very little fuss because there were no close relatives to mourn and no money for anything other than a simple burial.

'Certain constitutions,' said Margaret, 'do not last five minutes in India, and it is cruel to bring them out here.'

Sir Josiah Coatsworth sent a message of condolence and was so kind. He helped with the papers to enable Helen to remain in Calcutta. He sent over his own servants to assist her in managing Claire's few things and in writing to her relatives in England, even sending a form of words to use. He could not have done more and yet he did. He came to visit Helen and reassured her that, as the Major was in the north and was said to be distraught, she only needed to ask for anything at all. He was hers to command.

Claire's burial was without ceremony and without her husband, but she was truly mourned. Helen found herself crying at the grave, which made her quite cross. The burial had taken place quickly because of the heat.

Margaret's household expanded into the top of the house once more. Helen and Esme were assimilated into the whole. It was almost as if Claire had not existed. The Major appeared three weeks later and proposed that his child should remain where she was for the present. This suited little Esme, who was by now very attached to both Helen and Rani, her young ayah.

The Major was clear that he would stay with his regiment and could not countenance caring for a child himself. He did not appear to mourn his wife, only asking some matter-of-fact questions about which papers had been sent where regarding her death. He visited his child only twice, and during those visits did not conceal that he felt Sir Josiah had been somewhat high-handed. He did not, however, seek to revoke Coatsworth's generosity, and a short note after his second visit announced his departure from the district. Margaret was rather annoyed that he had not discussed the child or Helen's future at all. Helen reflected that Sir Josiah had shown more feelings for poor Claire and had understood her own frustration in spending days cooped up nursing an invalid. He had assured her that those days were over, and she would now have access to enjoyment and company.

Sir Josiah explained to Helen that of course Claire could not have survived.

'This,' he said, 'is India's way of separating the wheat from the chaff. It is the survival of the fittest. Her death should be accepted in order that ordinary life can resume'.

Sir Josiah agreed that regret was natural and it was perfectly understandable that Helen should feel relief when Claire died because nursing was too ugly and tedious a task for a lovely young person. He reassured her that this was not a question of selfishness, not at all. It was just that that life in India demanded a certain spirit of self-preservation. Sir Josiah added that Helen should not worry. She would not be forced to go home if she did not wish to do so. He also felt there was no reason why she should assume she would continue to care for the child. He said he felt her duties were completely discharged and she would need to consider her own plans for the future. Helen entirely agreed with him, and her spirits lifted.

Sir Josiah did not lose his opportunity. He proposed that there was now an urgent requirement for new diversion and fresh air. He suggested an early morning hunt on horseback, which would really set her up. Margaret vetoed this in the strongest possible terms, but Sir Josiah was not at all put out. He thought instead of how well suited he and Helen appeared to be.

Margaret was astonished by Sir Josiah's offer of assistance towards little Esme's keep and a corresponding amount to cover Helen's needs in the form of an allowance for an additional servant until the child was able to travel home to England. No time frame for this was specified. Margaret was somewhat perplexed by Sir Josiah's interest in the matter, especially as Helen's father had materialised and Margaret assumed *he* would assist Helen. Sir Josiah waved this away, insisting on helping – just until the Major was able to make his own arrangements. It was all agreed in a very brisk and matter-of-fact way. As it was her belief that a practical man should always be encouraged, Margaret accepted Sir Josiah's apparent kindness and, being very busy, thought no more about it.

A note from her father in November was the last thing Helen expected, but there was no avoiding him once it was delivered. The invitation to dine was worded in such a way as to leave her in no doubt that she was to leave Margaret behind. Instead she was accompanied by Badshah Raj.

As she was shown in to the two-storey house she observed children playing in the courtyard. They were not native children, for one of them had very fair hair. She conjectured that these must be the children of other Company officers. She was surprised, however, to see Sir Josiah Coatsworth present among the party. He did not stay long, making an excuse to attend another function. Helen thought his presence was unusual, but perhaps her father had been successful here after all. She thought, rather unkindly, that it would be the first success of his life.

The dinner consisted of an impressive number of courses. Helen was seated between a Captain Spencer, who was with a Sepoy regiment, and a Captain Grenfell, a military adviser to Sir Josiah. The conversation was limited, as both men seemed to be very preoccupied by the reduction in the *batta*. This was now in effect, causing them financial difficulty. They talked of little else in brief pauses between courses. Helen found she could not contribute anything more than sympathy as she did not understand what precious thing had been lost. She made a mental note to query this with Margaret, who seemed to know everything about military and Company life in Calcutta. Helen rose as the ladies retired, although it appeared this was for form's sake as the men quickly joined them.

Helen thought it odd when no tea arrived; rather the drinking continued in the presence of the ladies. She was seated at the far side of the room and her father sought her out, keen for the Company to see on what good terms father and daughter stood. It was then that he broached the idea of her going to live with him. He said that there was impropriety in continuing to live in the 'little hovel with the Scotswoman'. This drew a guffaw from the men present. Helen began to explain the very practical domestic arrangements, but her father was not listening. He pulled a large bolt of shimmering fabric from a bureau drawer.

'Make yourself a gown from this – and there's more where that came from.'

He draped the silken fabric around her. She pulled it from around her waist and he arranged it around her arms and shoulders. She could not refuse it in front of all the guests, but she could feel tight fabric and the oppressive heat in the room. She looked at him: his clothes were of the finest cloth, and the room was full of expensive furniture and ornaments. Helen realised he was now wealthy – but he was still vulgar. How could she accept gifts from this stranger, the man who had left her mother and herself without a word? Surely if anyone knew his history they would regard him differently.

Helen dearly wanted to leave, but she was determined to wait until the guests had gone. She wanted to make her father promise to send money home. She was tired and hot, and the company was loud. Helen was reminded of those noisy gatherings when she was younger. She wanted to return to the little whitewashed building where there was kindness and to Margaret, whom she could trust. However, there were things she must know, and she would not get a better chance to speak to her father. Helen needed to establish why he had left his regiment and come to India. When the last carriage had pulled away, she removed his arm from around her waist. She imagined he had put his arm around her to demonstrate to guests the loving relationship of a father and daughter long separated. Jennings shrugged.

'Well done, Helen. I am pleased. You behaved very well, my dear – not prone to outbursts like your mama. I had hoped you would follow my reasoning. I think that little show will do the trick. It could have been quite difficult, you popping up like this, but I have advised everyone that you have joined me in India as arranged and that your mother was too ill to travel. Now I think about it, Sylvia always was a bit sickly at sea. So, name the day. When would you like to move in? You can't want to stay with the Scot. I have every comfort here and you are quite the little hostess. I give very impressive dinners – it is part of the job, and you will be useful. What do you say?'

Helen was careful – she did not want to upset him before she got some answers. All she wanted to see was if, after all, he would do something for her mother at home.

Helen looked up at Jennings, linking his arm.

'Father,' she said in a soft voice. 'What is your role here and who pays for all this?' She waved her hand around the spacious room.

Jennings was surprised – this was not the response he had expected. She seemed a calm, sensible sort of girl and he saw no reason not to get better acquainted. It was only natural that she would be curious.

'I work, my dear, for the Company who bought me out very soon after I arrived here. Army life did not suit, as promotion is tediously slow. When I did a special favour for the Council in negotiations with ...' – he paused – '... well, no matter, it was a very special favour. I was handsomely rewarded, and now I give the orders. You do know, my dear, that to prosper we must make compromises. There are other ways of serving one's country – soldiers cannot do everything. The work I am engaged in enables essential trading. I safeguard arrangements to ensure we are able to sell our goods. I have a marvellous title; I am a 'Remembrancer', which means I negotiate vital business with the Chinese. It is difficult, not to say dangerous, work, but I am paid handsomely for my efforts. You are young, but I know that you understand I was not suited to life as an ordinary soldier.

'I arrange for the sale of our opium to China in quantity, and they supply us with tea and silk and other goods besides. Do not alarm yourself – this opium is very beneficial. It is taken for pleasure to soothe and calm. Why, it is almost medicinal and the making of it very clever.'

His eyes were shining as he spoke. He pulled from his pocket a sweet-smelling plug of brown gum. He allowed Helen to hold it, but she handed it back as her hands became stained and sticky.

'This,' said Jennings, rolling it between his fingers, 'is from the white poppy, which produces a greater yield. We prefer the white, although the purple flower is more beautiful. Purple is a lovely colour, is it not?' he observed, fingering the embroidered silk of the wall hangings.

Helen asked him to continue, as she was genuinely interested, and Jennings was only too happy to oblige.

'There are huge factories in the north, and the manufacture is secret and well secured. Just now the opium flowers are in bud in the fields, but they will ripen. They come to us at Patna in batches of one hundred jars. Each one is tightly sealed. If a pot is broken in transit, God help the native carrier, for there will be the devil to pay. You must know that the perfect flower is more valuable than silver. Security is of prime importance. I am one of the few with dispensation to avoid the constant searches.'

He lovingly fingered the glutinous, sweet-smelling lump. Helen noticed at this point that her father was wiping his wet mouth.

'We place an Englishman in charge of counting, weighing, assaying and checking each of the precious jars. There is great secrecy, hundreds of workers, and the science involved is astonishing. You would not believe the complexity of the testing and recording, weighing and measuring. Our customers are most exacting, so the goods must be perfect. If the opium is not pure, it will be found out and the sinful pot discovered. We need to make sure none of the opium sticks to the hands of the coolies or is wastefully left on the sides of the earthenware pots in which cakes are made.' Jennings smiled as he continued, 'You should see them, mere shadows of men at the river crawling like maggots among the shards of pot which are broken and thrown with the human rubbish into the Ganges'. He started to laugh. 'Some of the workers go bad and mad, no matter how skilled they have been. Once the poppy has them, they are no use to us.'

Jennings was full of energy, and his eyes shone as he described the process.

'You should see the workers in the factory, Helen, carefully making the opium cakes – oh so gently wrapping the petals around the lump. It is as if they were handling a small and precious child. Then, that careful laying-on of the final beautiful petal. This is the perfection that is the poppy cake. I am, I might say, indispensable, having developed our new security methods. We keep the opium cakes under double – no, triple – lock and key, and all the keys are in our safe. There is no way to get in or out undetected, and those who try to smuggle …'

He stopped, aware that Helen was looking at him. Her hands were clasped in front of her and, despite the stifling heat, she was pale. Helen felt such loathing; this man – her father – was almost drooling as he described his work. He had at last found a vocation, but what a vocation! Helen felt revulsion towards him but still she asked him to go on.

Jennings needed no encouragement and described how important he felt himself to be.

'The months of April, May and June are the farmers' busiest time. It is then that I treat with traders to fix the price. I have to keep an eye on them, for there are some thieves among them. I have come down heavily on their cheating practices. I will not tolerate theft, I will not allow it to go unpunished. A culture of fear is a powerful weapon. I am to return to my work very soon. I am not really required in the winter months until the packing starts, but I make it my business to meet with the traders in good time. I like to oversee the process in the factory during the late months to make sure all is well.

'We have to ensure the goods are carefully sewn into the mango chests. Mango is marvellous wood for keeping moisture, grubs and thieving fingers out. I tell you, girl, I have come into my own. I negotiate and treat with the Chinese. I ensure full payments are made before the goods leave our warehouses. I got us such a good price this year that I am consequently in very high favour with Sir Josiah. I stand before you, daughter, a success. You can write home if you like, tell your mother – which reminds me, I must send something home to her. I am doing well, and you know, my dear, that I am not heartless.'

He put an arm around Helen's shoulder and made to kiss her, but there was an indefinable smell on his body, his breath rancid. Helen pulled back, and her father smiled.

'Always the same, eh, Helen? There was a time when you would sit on your father's knee and kiss me, but I see all that has changed, and I know why. A fine husband he will make you. You are like me, Helen, you see the main chance and take it – good girl. He's older, to be sure, but I think you will not mind so much when he makes you Lady Coatsworth – and why should you, indeed? I shall certainly not stand in your way, in fact I will assist you by any means possible. You are my clever, clever girl!'

Helen turned and stared at him. She had remained calm while he gloated about his work, but now she was furious. She had listened to him because she wanted to understand why she and her mother had been abandoned. She heard herself screaming at him in a shrill voice.

'What do you mean? You actually think I would marry Sir Josiah? He is an old man. I would not accept him at any price. God knows why they bought you out, what you had to do to get out. Do not tell me, for I do not want to know. We have barely been able to live at home, mother and I. We have had neither clothes nor food. We have been reviled by complete strangers because of you, yet here you are in the lap of luxury without a thought for mother or me. You disgust me. I am ashamed of you and of my connection with you. I would do nothing – nothing – to aid or oblige you.'

Jennings was astonished at his daughter's reaction. But that did not matter, because he did not really care. This girl was the child of his former life, which had been humiliating and lowly. Now he had a fine house, a biddy and a new son. He only cared what people knew, so he needed to ensure this outburst was not repeated in public. It was better to let her scream and flounce here in his house with only his servants to hear.

Jennings placed the opium safely back in his pocket and turned to face Helen. He took her face in his hands. He was hurting her, but he had a strong grip and she could not get away.

'Understand this, daughter. Sir Josiah is obviously interested in you – his interest in you is the talk of Calcutta society. It is there for all to see except you, it seems. I expect you to take him seriously. He is wealthy beyond your imagination. You say I have provided you with nothing, but you are like me. I see it in you and you will not let this chance go. I would urge you, think carefully – he could buy you anything you want: jewels, a mansion, here or at home in England, for he must be due to go home soon. Sir Josiah just has to snap his fingers and he gets what he wants. You have only to appear interested in him and you have him. What you could possibly object to I cannot imagine. Do you want to be poor all your life?'

He let go of her.

'It is apparent from your reaction that you will not be accepting my hospitality. That is your choice, but I will not stand idle while you attempt to destroy my good reputation here. It has been an act of providence. I find myself in a favourable situation and I will not lose it. Do not attempt to harm me, whatever future you choose for yourself. I have made my choice – I will not go home to England.

This is my home now, and nothing must threaten my place here with the Company.'

Jennings felt that Sir Josiah's recent behaviour towards him must in part have been conditional on his daughter's eventual acceptance of a marriage proposal. He continued in a more soothing tone.

'You know that, were you to marry him, later you could have lovers your own age. If you were discreet, there would be no questions asked.'

Helen looked at him hard.

'You are very mistaken,' she stated. 'Sir Josiah is – that is to say, he appears to be – a fine man, but I love John Deuchars. I will have no one else as a husband. John is right-thinking and principled, but you would not understand what that is. Do you think that after all this time you have any influence over me? Do you think you deserve to have any authority over me or my life'?

Jennings snorted.

'I have heard of this John Deuchars; he is a juvenile. God knows why he was thought suitable for Patna – he could be dead of fever by now, for all I know.'

Helen froze.

'You know John?'

'A man in my position? Of course I don't know him,' replied Jennings. 'However, I saw him briefly on my last visit to the factory. Hopeless case, looked quite ill, no experience at all and saddled with the buffoon Mowbray, who I must soon remove.'

Helen turned away from him, and a small boy ran past her and leapt like a marmoset into his father's arms. He had large, oval eyes and spoke in a language unknown to her. He and his father looked at her; she noticed that they were perfectly alike. Helen had seen and heard enough, and made towards the door. Jennings shouted after her.

'Make a sensible choice, Helen, as I have done. Don't be the fool your mother was. Loving words and sentiment purchase nothing worth having in this world. Remember, whatever you do – do not cross me. I am still your father and you would be wise to let the world believe you are a dutiful daughter delighted to come out to join me.'

Daniel Jennings drew on a cheroot and laughed out loud. The sound of his laughter followed Helen out through the door and into the night, where Badshah Raj was waiting.

After his daughter had left, Daniel Jennings walked slowly from the bottom of his garden into the summerhouse. It was the last week in November and the evenings were cool. He lay down on a large outdoor sofa. He stroked the head of the small child, who was playing with his toy soldiers underneath a large palm. He had received news from his contacts in the north of possible trouble in Patna. The news was vague and unsubstantiated, but it was also ill-timed. It would attract attention to the factory and the complex negotiations underway with the Chinese. He sucked deeply on his pipe; he always felt so much more relaxed as he smoked. A myriad of thoughts competed against each other in his mind. He needed to be gone, needed to protect the trade which had been so lucrative for him. He drew deeply on the hookah and considered his options.

This boy John Deuchars was in the Patna district; it was he who had managed the processing of goods at Patna, with Mowbray. What could *they* do to counter any possible trouble, an idiot and a boy? He berated himself for not having reacted before now, but he had wanted to be sure of his daughter. The outcome of the evening had been less than satisfactory, and that annoyed him. Helen was no fool. He had remained behind to make sure of her discretion and as it was customary for a father to be asked for a daughter's hand. It would have been very gratifying to be asked by Sir Josiah for Helen's before he had to go north. Jennings was always ready to seize any opportunity and, with his own interests in mind, would pay a visit to Sir Josiah before leaving. It might pre-empt Sir Josiah to declare his intentions – it was worth a try. He would, of course, prefer the Deuchars boy out of the way to remove any inconvenience for Sir Josiah. Who could tell what mischief the boy had been up to? He could have yielded to temptation, like so many before him. Now that would be convenient.

As he smoked, he began to see John's removal as perfectly achievable. A good smoke always produced a plan. He would make sure of Sir Josiah and go immediately north. There were dangers everywhere in India just waiting for green and unwary young fools. He had worked for three years to build relationships with the Chinese traders and had made himself indispensable to the Company. He could not allow his interests to be jeopardised by sabotage. With informers everywhere, he could pursue the culprits whoever they were as soundlessly as a tiger stalks its prey. He would also manage his daughter's affairs whether she liked it or not, removing any and all impediment to his daughter's installation in the Coatsworth mansion. Jennings roughly pushed the small child away as he rose to his feet, and it began to cry.

It was dusk and the last of the light was disappearing fast as the smoke rose and curled from Jennings's pipe. He ground his teeth. *I will secure young John Deuchars inside the poppy. The petals will close on him as they have closed on so many others.* He smiled to himself as a servant helped him back to the house in a haze of delicious smoke.

Jennings was at Sir Josiah's door at eight the following morning. It appeared Sir Josiah had been expecting him, but that was the Superintendent's way with all his unexpected guests. Jennings found him eating heartily. Sir Josiah wiped his mouth with a napkin but did not look up as he spoke to the new arrival.

'I have something of a delicate nature which I need to discuss with you.'

This is it, thought Jennings. *He is going to ask me, Daniel Jennings, for my daughter's hand in marriage. I will be richer than I ever dreamed, for who will cross me when I am the father-in-law of Sir Josiah Coatsworth?*

'I would like you to go north, Jennings, and investigate some reports I have received,' Sir Josiah continued. 'I have troubling news about an incident in Patna. We may have lost something which belongs to the Governor-General and we must make shift to get it back.'

Jennings could hardly hide his disappointment, but said nothing. He bowed his head slowly, if only to conceal the annoyance that he could not now surprise Sir Josiah with the same information. Jennings pulled a letter from his coat pocket.

'Of course − I will make preparation to go immediately. In my absence, Sir, would you be so good as to see that my daughter receives this letter? There is no great urgency; perhaps in a number of days you might arrange for its delivery. I would rather this business is resolved before my daughter hears I am gone. She is headstrong, which is part of her appeal. When a father is so much from home … My lovely Helen requires some guidance. Her mother's influence was not all that it might have been. She is young and I am hopeful she will now be instructed by me as to appropriate choices for her future life. Until I return, I wonder if it would be presumptuous of me to ask you to act in my place. I am not convinced that her current accommodation or companions are entirely satisfactory.'

Sir Josiah smiled, as he responded.

'See if you can find out about the Deuchars boy. I hear your daughter is fond of him, as is my own. I also hear reports that he is mixed up in this inconvenient matter, but you know how unclear these messages from the north can be. I do need to know if he is acting the Company man or no. So many young men have, how shall we say, gone astray. I would prefer − that is to say, it would be preferable − if His Excellency the Governor-General were in ignorance for as long as it takes to put things to rights, if you follow my meaning. You will know what to do for the best, and you have, of course, my absolute confidence. Jennings, understand me when I say that I give you leave to manage what you find in Patna as you think fit, and I will make special effort to reassure your lovely daughter – will we not, my dear?'

There was a slight rustling sound from the window as Julia Coatsworth glided into the room from behind a large palm. She smiled and looked directly at Jennings. Julia knew her father wanted Jennings's daughter and was tolerating the horrible little man because of this. She also knew Jennings by reputation. She had heard enough of the conversation between the two men to know that John was in some sort of trouble. She could not doubt her father, as he would not condemn without evidence and he would always act quickly to guard his own interests. She understood that Sir Josiah was concerned that there could be potential for scandal. Any interruption in operations at Patna was unthinkable. Julia felt that he was very wrong to trust Jennings to resolve these matters, and she told him so. Sir Josiah was not in a mood to listen.

How, she thought, could her father even conceive that John was capable of doing anything wrong? She had been so pleased that John and her father had talked together. Julia knew that John Deuchars was an innocent, that he trusted people too much. He had a great deal to learn about the Company, yes – but 'unprincipled', never. Why, she thought, would he risk his reputation and bring shame upon the family he had so affectionately talked about? It would make no sense to do so. Jennings she knew well by reputation. She had heard rumours from the women in the house about his conduct, his spending and his debts. She was sure he was ruthlessly interested in his own fortunes. She was as surprised as anyone to hear that Helen was actually Jennings's daughter. Julia had been told by one of her maids that father and daughter had had a terrible fight and hated each other, but that was just town gossip.

After Jennings had left, she attempted again to share her concerns about him with her father. As he had done many times before when she tried to talk to him, Sir Josiah held up his hand to silence her. He bemoaned the fact that she had remained so long in India. When difficulty arose between them he always returned to the theme of his error in keeping such a daughter with him in India; that he should have sent her home to become an English lady like her mother, instead of letting her run wild. He also said that he had been neglectful in not securing female guidance for her, which was a new and disturbing theme.

Julia knew it was useless to argue with him when he was in this mood. She needed to find out more about the problems regarding Patna opium, but she would have to be careful. Her father would not like her asking questions in town and he would soon know if she did so, as he had informers everywhere.

If only Helen and she had become friends! But she reflected that, for some reason she could not immediately divine, they had not. Julia lay down in the heat of the day to consider how she must proceed. The stillness was punctuated only by the steady rhythm of the punkah wallah. Suddenly, she realised how stupid she had been – Helen and she had not become friends because of John Deuchars, who was in some sort of trouble at least two weeks' journey to the north.

Chapter Nine

It was early January 1830 and John was at last at leisure to review his time at Patna. He was exhausted. He had suffered all through the hot summer months preparing the factory for the poppy's arrival. He had no respite for weeks during the manufacture, and now all efforts were concentrated on packing. The last days – he could hardly say how many – he had endured an almost subterranean existence. Moving about from one godown to another he checked and counted, weighed and checked again. John supervised the packing and recorded the chests' individual seal markings. There were rules and instructions for everything. John had carried them through to the letter, working through each night. He had grown up somewhat in the last four months, the last two of which had been his worst.

It had been cooler during November and December, but more humid than was bearable as the climate had turned unseasonably moist. Day had merged into night as several of the weighment books had required rewriting due to the mould that devoured everything. John found himself falling asleep at his desk. He was jolted awake by the factory mantra: 'Each chest holds forty balls, each cake two seers, one and three-quarter chittaks all'. His responsibilities had required him to live within the factory, and he frequently could not eat, having spent so much time breathing in the sickly stench of the opium cakes, stacked in *jettas* of 500 each. He had continual headaches, which he put down to endless writing, checking and re-checking in the airless godowns.

Mr Mowbray had found his services very useful. He said that John had enabled him to contemplate going back to Mrs Mowbray alive. He praised John for his diligence and was apologetic that his digestive ill-health had rendered him unable to superintend. These apologies came in the shape of little notes with instructions attached. Mr Mowbray was always mistaken in his grasp of progress made and work remaining. The instructions, invariably arriving post the procedures to which they related, had been of no practical use. The last message from his mentor had reminded John that the value of one chest of forty balls was 18,000 rupees, or £250, and that John should make sure the guards were especially vigilant. This information only made John more anxious and he shook as he destroyed the note according to Mowbray's diktat. They had waited for the westerly winds, which had come late in early November, to pack the last shipment. All the balls, with their iridescent leaves, were nestled in poppy trash to minimise crushing. They had then been placed in chests, ready for transport. That was two long days before; now the chests were completed and stacked high in the godowns. John saw the dark, forbidding pile and wished fervently that they were en route to China.

John estimated that, at the current rate of progress, this would be two days thence. He could not understand the delay. He had seen Daniel Jennings, who had taken issue with everything John had said and screamed at him for no reason. He had asked questions about security to which John had not known the answers, and flatly refused to seek out Mr Mowbray for clarification, as John suggested. Jennings had left in a foul temper, disappearing into the hills to agree prices with the incoming traders. John was advised by Mr Mowbray that Jennings was always tetchy when so close to a sale and he should not worry. Once the chests were off their hands, they would be able to rest easy before returning to Calcutta. Mr Mowbray said: 'Spring and summer months are our own. The money is in the bank. Above all thanks to you, my boy, I shall live.'

Mr Mowbray had appeared very briefly at the factory. He satisfied himself that there was a large enough mountain of papers to prove to anybody that, at eight times throughout the day for weeks, the stores had been checked. When Mr Mowbray had completed a review of the records he said that it was clear that waste and pilfering had been reduced to a negligible amount. John said that he had introduced additional searches as some of the coolies would attempt to smuggle opium grains under their armpits. He had also instigated checks for counterfeit identification checks to make sure that the oval metal discs issued to all workers were genuine.

Mr Mowbray appeared very pleased with the improved security, applauding John's continuous presence at the factory. He had also sent letters to the Home Secretary in his name as Factory Superintendent, detailing the new innovations and improvements. In these, Mowbray had omitted any mention of John's name. The process, he advised in his letter to Sir Josiah, had been 'as tight as a poppy bud itself'. Now all the chests, in their gunny bags, were under guard. He remarked to John that the magnitude of responsibility in guarding a consignment valued at one million pounds sterling was in itself enough to kill a man. Mr Mowbray, as was his habit, returned to the comfort of his bungalow in time for dinner.

John had not imagined that this would be his role in the management of India. He could not bring himself to write much about his work in letters to those at home. Mr Mowbray had said that that was nonsense; he should certainly report home that his work was important to the Company and, therefore, to the country. He added that any parent would be sensible and see the value of his efforts. Did his parents not enjoy their tea like everyone else?

However, John had seen the human cost, in the form of wrecked lives on the banks of the Ganges – wasted, vacant faces, sucking at shards of pot half-concealed in the mist – and knew his parents would not regard it in the favourable terms suggested by Mowbray.

He also knew he must make the best of it. He made a note to speak to the Company men on the boats to finalise arrangements for loading. He would urge them to make sure the *churrundars* remained wide awake.

It was the day before the chests began their journey, and Mr Mowbray sent word that he absolutely must see John before the final loading to give him important and detailed instructions. John found that these related more to Mr Mowbray's minor financial interests along the river than to factory business. It seemed that Mowbray wanted to make sure of his river fees on the return journey; he wanted John to secure additional supplies from the remaining factory stores to sell on the route home.

John sat in a low sedan and sipped his tea; it was scalding hot and sweet. He looked out into the dusty street and watched as a small boy coaxed a huge buffalo along with a switch. The child stamped his feet and screamed in a high-pitched little voice, running from one side of the road to the other. The animal refused to cooperate, and an old woman cackled in amusement, which only made the child cross. John knew how the boy must feel; the animal was like India – moving at its own pace, no matter what.

On this particular evening, John had ridden reluctantly to the bungalow as soon as he had finished in the factory, as Mr Mowbray had instructed. He hoped to return after he had spoken to him. The older man was bored and absolutely insisted that John stay the night to discuss the season's crop. He wanted to go over the security arrangements and the route of their return journey to Calcutta. Mr Mowbray also said that, despite fragile health, it was a habit of his to watch the chests leaving. It would not be correct to leave this final act to John. He said that he and John could just as easily set off for the factory early the following morning.

Morning arrived, but there was no sign of Mr Mowbray. The heat was creeping into the day. He was, in fact, taking a refreshing bath, but appeared in time to sit down to a rather fine breakfast. All John could think about was getting back to the factory, as he had received a message late in the evening that Daniel Jennings had not arrived with the traders as expected to oversee the handover and they would not take the goods without his signature. In a hurried note, John had already instructed Amil, the overseer, to send a message to summon Jennings. John was aware that it would look very bad indeed if Jennings eventually arrived at the factory and neither the Factory Superintendent nor his assistant were present and the traders were thus in the compound unsupervised.

It was after a frustratingly long breakfast, just as they were about to leave for the factory, that the response came through. Mr Mowbray was seated in his palanquin in the shade of the bungalow and making an enormous fuss about his curtains. The messenger ran screaming into the quiet garden. He fell wide-eyed to his knees in front of Mr Mowbray, and told him that there had been a robbery at the factory. Preliminary investigations had revealed that there had been three explosions the previous evening, which had started a fire setting light to the walls of the godowns. John came running at the sound of a commotion in the garden, to be told that the godowns were still burning.

The frantic messenger said that the fire had taken quickly. It had spread from the rush mats on the red-brick floors into a section of the roof. He said that they had been unable to get in to put out the fires because the mango wood chests had been heaved in front of the door and set alight. Once the fires had taken, the blaze had been too intense. The two guards posted at the entrances of three of the godowns had been found strangled in the bottom of an alligating vat, and the door to the storage area was found wrenched off its large hinges. John listened in disbelief as the messenger said that in one of the godowns the fires had not taken, but a large number of chests inside were found to have been broken open and their contents removed. Hundreds of poppy cakes were missing. The traders were in the compound, creating riot and threatening to leave.

In another of the godowns, a hole had been found hewn through the side wall nearest the river. The sepoys posted at each of the godowns on the riverside were dead, their strangled bodies dragged down the bank. There were, John was told, cart tracks and footprints to the river, and at the river's edge raffia baskets had been found floating in the water, close to the bodies of the river guards. This, said the breathless messenger, was some hours ago.

Mr Mowbray fell back prostrate against his cushion, his chest heaving as he gasped for breath. John fetched water, concerned at Mowbray's irregular breathing. He tried to reassure him.

'Please, sir, do not concern yourself. I will go back to the factory and see what must be done. You cannot go, as you are not fit to travel.'

John wondered why the factory staff had wasted valuable time before sending a runner, given the seriousness of the incident. He cursed the absence of the semaphore, which had been talked about but not yet installed. John could not expect to get a message to Calcutta in less than a week. All his dreams of returning to the lovely Julia were shattered.

John saddled his mare and set off in the blazing heat. He rode flat out without stopping, arriving at the factory after noon. He found the whole compound full of smouldering debris. A dozen people tried to talk to him at once. The fires had created much smoke and a sweet, acrid smell hung in the air. The far wall of one of the godowns was found to be unsafe as the lower section had collapsed. There was so much confusion. The red-brick floor was blackened by the remains of the fires and covered in hot ash.

It was obvious from the broken baskets and boxes strewn about that opium cakes were missing, but worse was to follow. The fire had contaminated the remaining stock. Shards of pots lay scattered everywhere. The discipline which John had introduced and maintained had completely broken down; he could see none of the guards. It was evident that other pillaging had followed in the aftermath of the robbery, and people were still running about trampling over the scene. Pots of opium were lying on their side. The glutinous brown treasure was melting into the ground before his eyes. John pushed through the frantic workers and in the midst of a crowd of screaming people found Amil.

Amil Gouind Ram was a capable man who had been of great service to John throughout the preparations for shipment. It was he who had organised the initial dampening down of the fires in the early morning. He had now placed the bodies of the dead guards in a neat row in the shade, ready for burning. They would have to be moved soon. Amil had assembled as many of the frightened people together as he could, but it was a fraction of the workforce. Many were so terrified they had disappeared into the countryside. John began to speak to the remaining workers. They all looked at him with wide eyes in smoke-blackened faces. He could see others walking quietly out of the compound with bundles under their arms, but was powerless to stop them.

Amil was not his usual self. John asked if he had seen anything before the fires began, but he looked away. None of the workers were prepared to say much, and what they did say was not helpful. There were tales of giants rampaging through the walls of the godowns. People said it was the furious god Shiva taking her vengeance on the opium devil. The only interesting piece of information related to an unknown man who had been seen talking with the guards at the compound gates earlier in the evening of the robbery. John sent off a message to head office in Calcutta asking for assistance, but did not mention the report of the stranger or the apparent delay in alerting Mr Mowbray or himself.

Amil informed John that he had arranged for the message to be delivered to Sahib Jennings calling on him to urgently return to the factory and wondered why John had sent another note advising Sahib Jennings to follow a group of horsemen sighted in the hills who might be a threat to the legitimate traders. Amil said he imagined Sahib Jennings did not know about the robbery and that his fury would be terrible.

John had obeyed Mr Mowbray and gone to the bungalow, he had sent one note only to Daniel Jennings urging him to come to the factory. Now there was total devastation, John felt helpless. Without Jennings and his men he could not organise a search for the thieves. His knowledge of the area and its people was very limited. He had sent a runner to Mowbray advising him of the situation and asking for guidance, but had received no reply.

Daniel Jennings, meanwhile, had found a small party of the traders quietly waiting for the rest of their baggage train to return with the caravan of chests. All was quiet in the hills. Jennings was no fool and immediately turned his horse around. As he neared Patna, he could smell the damage before he saw it. In one of his villages he was told of a white sahib who had planned to plunder the factory. No persuasion had been necessary to secure this information; these villagers knew Daniel Jennings, and he was not to be crossed. At his side was a man whose reputation was useful when men were reluctant to talk. The hills bred hard, uncompromising men. Those beautiful and wild hills had bred Shuja, but they had not formed him – the Company did that. He had previously owned no land of his own but had assisted the Company in forcibly taking his neighbours' lands for opium cultivation by discrediting them. He was rewarded for his services by being made a 'Zamindar', a landlord in his own right, and by this means he increased the area of land for opium cultivation and, in the process, his own wealth. He also accumulated money by bribing and extorting farmers hoping to avoid losing their land. When they were no longer able to pay him, he heaped on them accusations of alleged non-payment of taxes and rents due to the Company. He had used any means he could, including allegations of witchcraft, to wrest good growing land from local farmers. He did not work alone; although hated and feared, he was well guarded, and too powerful to challenge because it was perceived he had the support of the British.

After a day of exhausting clearing-up at the factory and mounting frustration, John was relieved and pleased to see Jennings riding into Patna. He hoped that together they might salvage something from the mess. Amil had been quiet but diligent and John was grateful for his help. John reasoned that Amil, usually so talkative, was quiet due to the shock of the robbery and the back-breaking work of clearing the site. John had already had to deal with a number of angry Chinese merchants and – unable to give them the reassurances they required – he begged them to wait for Jennings or Mowbray who, he said, were due at any time. In any case they could surely see for themselves that their expected cargo of precious opium was ruined. Their hand gestures and demeanour made it clear that they were angry at the prospect of leaving empty-handed.

John recognised Shuja riding alongside Jennings. He was Jennings's self-important eyes and ears in Patna district. Loathed by peasants and workers alike, he was well rewarded by Jennings. He and Jennings had a long-standing relationship and had already spoken at length on their way back to the factory. Forming in Jennings's mind was the very clear impression of who might be responsible for the robbery. Jennings had not exactly named the man, but Shuja was no fool. He knew exactly how Sahib Jennings's mind worked. After all, reasoned Jennings out loud, 'Who was it who encouraged him to go upriver and get him and his men out of the way?' The message he had received was from none other than John Deuchars, handed to him by the overseer Amil.

Jennings had been made to look a fool. The trail was now cold and, as he listened to the report of the robbery, he visibly shook with anger. He should have come north sooner; he would have rooted out Deuchars' plans. He had ignored his own first rule: business before pleasure. He could not blame his network of spies and contacts throughout the villages, who had done their job. He could only blame himself. Then, like an idiot, he had rushed out into the countryside, while the robbery took place. It was too much to bear.

Oblivious to all reason, Jennings was consumed by rage, incredulous at his own stupidity. Encouraged by Shuja and the angry traders, he rode into the compound and ordered the seizure of Amil. John was close to the ensuing commotion and saw that Amil was held fast by three strong sepoys. John could see Jennings on his horse, but he could not make him hear above the commotion. He pushed his way through the crowd. Exhausted, he could not remember when he had last slept, but he rushed up to Jennings, who had dismounted.

'What is the meaning of this?' he demanded. 'What are you doing? Have you gone mad? This man is innocent. What do you want with him? Of what is he accused?'

Jennings turned to John.

'He is accused of being party to a theft, Mr Deuchars. He is involved in the organisation of this outrage.'

Jennings gestured to the wreckage of the factory.

'We will have names out of him before the day is over, names of all his accomplices.'

John moved to intervene, but his way was blocked and Jennings held his arm.

'You would be wise to step back, Mr Deuchars.'

The officious Zamindar Shuja led the way, pushing aside everyone in his path, smiling importantly while beating Amil around the legs with his stick. Amil was taken shouting to the guard house. Jennings was in a hurry and Amil apparently uncooperative, so it did not take long for Shuja to begin applying hot irons to his buttocks and feet. John could hear his screams but could do nothing to help him.

John attempted to leave the factory compound but was prevented by Jennings's men. It was late afternoon when Shuja persuaded a bloody Amil to name John Deuchars as the leader of the Patna thieves. Jennings lost no time in seizing a surprised and indignant Deuchars and placing him under house arrest. Jennings was satisfied with his day's work, but he was not finished. He needed to consolidate. As dusk fell, he went in search of Mowbray.

Hugh Mowbray lay prostrate in his bungalow outside the town. Jennings explained to him the seriousness of the situation with the Chinese and the regrettable events of the day concerning his assistant, John Deuchars. He did so in a voice full of poignant regret.

Mowbray was silent, and then his eyes filled with tears.

'Oh, my dear Lord,' he said. 'Jennings, I am shocked. We have so many checks and everything secure to prevent just this sort of thing. Everyone has their tickets, all metal, you know, and so finely made. Surely it was impossible for anyone to get into the factory without detection by the department Sirdar.' He hesitated and then, in a whisper, added, 'But then there is subterfuge, I suppose. These young fellows come out here and the temptation is far too great. I try to mentor them, you know. I try to keep the arrow straight, but what more can I do for them that I have not done? You will believe me when I tell you that I have spent hours tutoring John Deuchars. Now you tell me that this is my reward. I have the most fearful luck with these young men, I must say. You tell me he sent a message to you which implied danger in the hills and the factory was left unguarded. Surely your spies know a genuine message from a false one – but no matter, it is done.

'The last one, poor boy, smelt the flower and that was that. I tell you without fear or favour, India killed him. She takes them young, very young. I am amazed that I have survived this long. I learned this through the long years when I asked for little and worked like a slave for the Company. My own sort of dedication is rare now, but no matter. I will write to his mother and father, of course. I wrote a very similar letter to a farmer's wife in Northumberland only two years ago.'

He recalled his letter of sympathy, perfectly crafted for the occasion. He pursed his full lips and reached for his handkerchief. Mr Hugh Mowbray could be relied upon to hit just the right note of regret and sorrow. He turned towards Jennings, eyes brimming with tears.

'How many jettas do you suppose have been taken? More than one hundred? More than one thousand? No, do not tell me!'

Mowbray's face was hidden, his handkerchief pressed across his eyes.

'Leave me now, so I may compose myself. I should avoid strong emotion – my doctors say it will be the death of me.'

Jennings knew that the letter he had received from John Deuchars would place him in heavy disgrace. John would be tried and there would be no chance of reprieve. While John Deuchars rotted in a Company prison cell, Helen would marry Sir Josiah. It was really very satisfactory – he had not been required to do anything to bring about the boy's ruin. Jennings was under no illusion that the culprits had been found. He knew this was not the work of a mere boy. This robbery had required an intimate and detailed knowledge of the area that John Deuchars could not possess – but who would know that? The Company would not ask awkward questions; Sir Josiah did not want to know what happened in the field. In fact, nobody wanted to talk about poppy factories at that moment, as long as they quietly continued to produce the goods. All that would be publicly known was that John Deuchars had spent hours alone at the factory; that his family were impoverished compared to their former state; and that temptation had been too great. This explanation would be enough to furnish the Company with the scapegoat it needed.

Jennings also knew that the real culprits would never be caught. They had been given too much time to get away. The Company would want this mess cleared up with as little fuss as possible. After all, it must not be said that the Company could not run its affairs in India. There was already too much damaging criticism at home. Government interference in Company affairs would restrict Daniel Jennings's opportunities for improvement, and that he could not allow. The difficult task of finding the real thieves would be conducted in secret. Jennings knew he would need to restore his credibility violently at night in the villages. He and Shuja would find out who the culprits were but it would take time. Meanwhile, John Deuchars would serve his purpose.

The Company did not want to know what he actually did; they just wanted the unsavoury jobs done. It was quite obvious that the buffoon Mowbray would be no help at all. How, Jennings wondered, had such a pathetic little man been given any responsibility at all? He reflected that he might have connections on the Board – that was the usual way to advance in the Company. Reflecting on this did not improve his mood. Late in the afternoon, after an angry interview with his Chinese traders and just as the sun was setting, Jennings sent his sepoys to John's living quarters. John was marched through the factory compound so that all could see the guilty man.

Jennings was in a savage frame of mind. He ground his shoe into the ash at his feet and spat cheroot-coloured saliva onto a pile of smouldering debris. It had been a scorching day and there was still no news as to the whereabouts of the missing goods. The robbers had apparently disappeared into thin air. The locals were silent; no one appeared to know anything. In the interview that followed, John was made to understand that Amil was near death. He was accused of assisting in the theft of a huge quantity of opium. John was told that that Amil had confessed to being his accomplice.

John was incredulous, and turned on Jennings.

'What do you mean, "accomplice"? We have been here, both of us, trying to restore order. How could you imagine that I would – *could* – organise such a thing?'

'You are,' said Jennings, 'quite the innocent, then. You send me a note to say there have been sightings of thieves in the hills to delay my arrival. Then you appear at the factory having been absent when the robbery was taking place. How very convenient. Then you stay and play the Company hero, ordering the workers, coordinating the clearing of the mess. Meanwhile, your accomplices have taken the Company's property who knows where. No, I say your action evidences remarkable cunning. For all I know, you have been covering your tracks and those of your accomplices. Do not think your air of innocence fools me. You had better make a clean breast of the whole thing. Who was it that sent me miles into the hills? It was you, Deuchars. You and your damned message!'

'You are mad!' responded John. 'I was with Mowbray on the night of the robbery. Ask him – he will tell you I was with him. In fact, he insisted on my going to him, or I would not have left the factory. I sent no note advising you to leave the factory to look for robbers in the hills. Now I insist that you take me to Amil. Take me to him!' shouted John. 'Take me to Amil.'

Jennings smiled, blowing the smoke of his cheroot into John's face.

'Do you have any conception of the damage done here? We may never repair it. A whole year of trade with the Chinese is almost ruined; you have brought about that ruin. You have also inconvenienced me, and I will see you punished for it. You say that you were with Mowbray. Well, I have seen Mowbray and he never once mentioned to me that you were with him at all. No, by God, you were out there …' – Jennings gestured to the low scrub and trees outside the compound – '… waiting for your chance.'

Jennings was speaking to the crowd, which stood quietly. He motioned to the guards, who turned John round and marched him towards the strongroom. The door was ajar, and as they entered John could hear moaning. He was pushed roughly down a dark hallway as two of the guards followed. Amil was lying against the wall, his white leggings soaked with blood, his mouth cut and swollen. He saw John and made a painful move towards him.

'I had to say it, sahib – they would have killed me,' he cried.

He held out his fingers, which were mashed almost to jelly at their tips. Two of the fingers of the right hand were missing. Far more serious were the wounds to his groin and buttocks, which made movement excruciating.

'They made me tell them that you came to the godown with your men. I would not have said it, but they have unmanned me.'

Amil shook, sobbing convulsively. He reached out and touched John's hands, leaving them wet and bloody.

Amil's voice was now only a whisper but John heard him say, 'I know you must have had your reasons, sahib'.

Jennings heard too.

'You see, Mr Deuchars, your accomplice is unable to tell a lie. At least he knows what truth is.'

A guard kicked Amil in the chest and he fell backwards. John lunged at the guard but was pulled upright, his arms pinned behind him. The other guard pushed him back towards the door. John was shaking with anger and turned to Jennings.

'This is an outrage! You have done this dreadful thing to an innocent and I will see you in prison for it.' Turning his head to Amil, he shouted, 'Believe me, friend, I am not responsible for this. I do not know what they mean, but don't worry, I will come back for you.'

Amil's bloodied hand reached towards John again and then dropped.

'Sahib, forgive me and forget me – my life is finished.'

Jennings sneered and turned to the guards.

'Yes, yes, Mr Deuchars, very touching. Guards, Take him away.'

John, now desperate, had a wild thought that if he could just escape and get back to Mowbray, he would vouch for him. He struggled in the arms of the sepoys and shouted at Jennings.

'This is insane! What do you mean by all this? What motive could I have here? I know few people in this area and I do not speak enough of the language. I came as soon as I had news. I sent you no message to go to the hills. Why do you believe this of me?'

Why he panicked, John could not afterwards say. It may have been the darkening western sky or the looming shapes of the blackened godowns. It might have been rage at the mutilation of Amil or just his total sense of isolation from any form of assistance. His head swam and he felt sick but, as Jennings had hoped, John did what he should not have done.

He took a chance and pulled himself free of the two sepoys. He knew it was hopeless. He had been on the point of running from this place, from the job, from India. Now it was almost an instinctive reaction, his chest bursting as he ran for his life. He could hear them coming as the blood pounded in his temples. The hot and smoky evening air burned his throat. He knew that he could not outrun them. He had nowhere to hide and no plan. A sob rose in him as he remembered his lovely Julia. Regardless of the hopelessness of his situation, he felt that he could not have stood and listened to Jennings's sneering and accusations a moment longer.

John did not understand why this was happening to him, but he couldn't think of that now. His only chance lay in getting to the river. It was twilight and as he ran he tried to make a plan. If he could only outrun them, he could wait until darkness fell and somehow get to the water and a boat. As he thought about his chances on the river, he lost his footing on the rough ground and fell heavily. Aware of searing pain in his hands and legs, he tried not to cry out. He felt the hot, stabbing shards of a broken pot cutting into his legs. He got to his feet, alternately crouching and running under the cover of the river bank. He slowed to get his bearings; the undercut bank was some distance from the water. At intervals there were rocky overhangs, covered with weeds and roots. He hid for a time under the vegetation while he made an effort to pull a large shard of pot out of his shin. Even here there was the sweet stench that he knew so well. John recognised the place; he had watched the poor scraping out the broken pots, sucking at them after the rain. John lay against the hot sand as beetles crawled across his arms and neck. He waited for what seemed like hours, listening to the sounds on the river and the crickets in the grass. He could hear the shouts of his pursuers in the distance, but he kept his eyes on the river. The sky seemed to meet the water, which appeared blood-red reflecting the light of the dying sun. The huge ball hung above the water and John remembered part of a poem.

Look out into the streaming sun, that shining river of sea,
Cast me in on a clear day, it will take me away ...

It seemed to John to be about leaving and loss, but he couldn't remember any more. The words in his head repeated and echoed.

He was hot and felt sick; his limbs were throbbing and heavy, as if made of lead. He thought he heard English voices, his sister's laughter and the smell of the rose garden at home. Thoughts of home did not help, and panic rose inside him once more as he crouched alone. He considered that he might die in this place, and nobody would know of the injustice. He would be shamed, and his family would be forced, unbelieving and sorrowful, to accept his disgrace and death. Then he thought of his Julia and willed himself to stay calm, to fight his way out. He would not submit to this – he would use the anger welling up as a weapon.

John knew he must make a move before he was found. He eased himself into a better position so that he could scan the water's edge. In the half-light it was difficult to make out where the river bank ended and the water began. He crawled out from under the concealing rock and, despite his injuries, made his way towards the sound of lapping water. In the last of the light he saw a low, dark shape ahead. Slowly he made his way towards it, hoping against hope that it was a small boat. His heart was raging in his chest; the pain in his legs made him stumble. In the same moment he made a dash for the water, the shape rose up from the shore and he ran straight into the arms of a sepoy.

Chapter Ten

Helen was dressing young Esme when she became aware of a purposeful step on the stairs. There was a rap at the door, and Major McLennan entered before she had time to say 'come'. Helen pulled little Esme towards her and gently whispered: 'It's alright, darling – it's your father'. The little girl shied away and hid under Helen's skirts.

The Major did not seem to notice the child.

'I am come to advise you that I go to Bombay, I do not know for how long. You seem to have things in order here, but when I return you shall go home with Esme. I will make arrangements for you to take her to my mother. Until then I should be obliged if you would carry on as before. I believe financial arrangements are in place, although I can ill afford you. If you practise economy, I cannot think one child will cause much trouble. In any event, I cannot give you more since they removed the *batta*, which purchased all the extras. We are all practising economy now, don't you know?' He seemed momentarily distracted. 'Things are not as I had hoped they would be. Damned foolish idea, coming out here. Stupid childish notion to bring girls to this place, but it cannot be mended now.'

At last, thought Helen, *he has mentioned his wife – and after all this time.* She looked into his eyes as she spoke.

'Claire was very determined to come to you and she was so brave, despite being very poorly. She told me that she did not want to remain in England without you.'

Helen did not seek to comfort him; she felt he did not really deserve it. She wanted to make him see that he had been a poor sort of husband. She wanted to explain to him what a devoted wife he had lost. The Major stared at her and almost sneered.

'Oh that – no, it was not of her I spoke. I meant the children; Claire was a fool to bring them out when she should have left them with my mother, as arranged. What was she thinking, that I needed infant daughters out here? A man might tolerate daughters of a personable age if there is a son, but where is my son? She might have brought me an heir, that would have served; a man likes to shape a son, but not a daughter. She did not provide me with a son and that is bad form.' He looked briefly at Esme, who had emerged from beneath Helen's skirts, and snorted, 'I suppose she may become interesting and require my attention when she is seventeen and a husband is called for. Until then she would have been as well with my mother – it is all vastly inconvenient.'

Helen stared; he seemed not to have heard anything she had said. Major McLennan was impatient to leave.

'I have taken enough of your time and must soon sail for Bombay. I must also see Sir Josiah about the business in Patna, which sounds more serious than I had first thought.'

Helen started and asked immediately what he meant. The Major was brusque in ordinary conversation but relaxed when drawn to talk about his regiment. He described how, coming down from the north, he had heard of rumours of trouble at Patna. There had been some kind of riot. His orders had been to return to Calcutta and so he had not detoured. There were now stories circulating of something more serious.

'In ordinary circumstances the factories do not interest me,' he advised Helen while pacing the floor. 'I am a soldier, not a factory guard. I do not chase after dacoits unless wholly necessary. I have absolutely nothing to do with trade.'

Then, reflecting on the thought that he had possibly erred in not taking his regiment to Patna, the frown returned, and he made his excuses and left. He as good as instructed Helen to stay where she was, saying he would book passage for his child when he returned. He did not kiss Esme, who was now playing with a rush doll in a corner of the room. *How*, thought Helen, *could someone so gentle have loved such a man?*

The Major had referred to trouble in Patna but said nothing clarifying or helpful. Having paced the room worrying about what the trouble might be, Helen suddenly thought of someone who would surely know. She felt that the Major was bringing old news and wanted to determine if the rumour was true and if there was any news of John. Sir Josiah had said that she might call at any time and would always be welcome. Margaret would have advised that she should send a servant to enquire if it would be convenient to call. Helen preferred a more personal approach, and hoped that she would not encounter Julia.

Sir Josiah was at home and was very kind. He made her sit down with a cup of very sweet tea. She liked this man, who seemed careful of people. Importantly, he did not treat her like a child. When she asked about Patna he became grave but not dismissive.

'My dear,' he began, 'there has been, it is true, an unforeseen problem – an incident of sorts – in that district, but not a riot, so do not distress yourself.'

Helen was not distressed – she just wanted information.

'We must have confidence, Helen,' Sir Josiah continued, 'because it is your own very capable father who has gone to manage the situation. Therefore we have nothing to fear.'

This intelligence froze Helen to her chair. She was not at all reassured – in fact quite the reverse. She tried to appear calm.

'There is,' said Sir Josiah, 'one piece of news for which I think you must prepare. It will be common knowledge in the town very soon because bad news travels faster than good.'

Helen started.

'No, do not fear, your father is not harmed. This is an unpleasantness which I cannot conceal, and it is best that you hear it from a friend. Believe me when I say that none of his behaviour reflects upon you, at least not in my eyes. There are some, of course, who may not feel as I do when it comes to the behaviour of ones family, but you know you have friends here who will not shun you.'

Sir Josiah made an attempt to catch Helen's hand. She moved, but not quickly enough. As she had noticed before, Sir Josiah was very agile for an older man; he held her fast. His hands were cool, and she could feel a strong pulse.

'Your cousin, my dear lady, has been arrested. He has allowed himself to become involved in criminal activity, no doubt lured by the promise of riches. I am afraid there is no way of breaking this to you gently. He has been charged with corruption and theft on an unprecedented scale.'

Sir Josiah said this with sympathy evident in his voice, leaning towards Helen and watching for her reaction. She unsuccessful attempted to take back her hand; Sir Josiah strongly resisted. He was annoyed that she had not swooned, which would have been so pleasant. *What*, he thought, *is the matter with young ladies today?*

'Please rest assured that I will ensure justice is done,' Sir Josiah continued. 'Your young cousin will not be harmed before his case is heard. I will make enquiries as to the exact nature of the charges, but they are of a very serious nature. I own, I am surprised at his behaviour,' Sir Josiah mused, almost to himself. 'That such a young man should be capable of aiding these thieves from inside Company premises and with all the security measures which I know to be in place. Mowbray is fastidious; I am persuaded that security is not the issue.'

Helen was aware of a stillness in the room. She was cold, and shook slightly. Retrieving her hand, she asked Sir Josiah very quietly: 'What actual evidence is there against John Deuchars?'

Sir Josiah tried to take hold of her hand again but failed.

'There are, it grieves me to say, witnesses,' he continued in a pained tone. 'He and his accomplices seem to have planned this throughout the processing of this year's stock. We can overlook very small entrepreneurial activities, my dear. There has always been some small trade among employees, however careful the Company is in matters of security. This is another matter altogether. We cannot conceal a theft of this scale.' Sir Josiah was in earnest as he continued, 'Thousands of pounds-worth of goods are missing and there is the matter of the complete destruction of our facilities. I am so sorry, Helen – India will lead those with a weak and wicked disposition away from their duty. I can only repeat that I have sent your father, the capable Mr Jennings, to discover the truth.'

Helen asked for a moment alone; Sir Josiah obliged and wandered into the conservatory.

He tried very hard to imagine that this boy had masterminded such a raid. He was advised by trusted employees that the evidence was overwhelming. He found John personally agreeable; he reminded him of himself as a young man. It could not be denied that John could have been a small impediment to his own suit. Any fool could see that she was half in love with him, but love was not everything. He was confident that, given time, he could persuade her that life with him, a knight of the Realm, would have its attractions. And the more he considered this matter, the more convinced he was that John Deuchars had nothing whatsoever to do with this dreadful robbery.

The news changed everything, and with remarkably little effort on his part. Deuchars was ruined and no longer a threat. He knew that it would be more convenient for him if this John were discredited. Sir Josiah felt that no young woman or sensible father would take Deuchars as husband or son-in-law after this. It would put paid to any silly ideas Julia had entertained about him. He intended Julia to marry into money or a title – she was pretty enough. In the darker recesses of Sir Josiah's mind, he now had a clear field. What a shame it was – John had been good company; but there would be other young men. Sir Josiah could not help but reflect that Indian prisons were not very conducive to good health. It was likely that John would end up in one. He did not mention this to Helen; contrary to popular belief, he did possess a heart.

Sir Josiah cared very much about the breach of security. The repercussions of such a scandal and the loss of income were a major concern. What would Sir Alfred Venables, the Governor-General, say? Sir Josiah would need to let him know some of the detail, but it would be hushed up, as these things always were. The whole affair could be blamed on local *thagi*. He and the Governor-General would decide on a suitable version of events. Sir Josiah had been deep in thought but became aware that Helen had followed him.

'I am sorry, my dear. Let me order some tea. Now, where were we? I entrusted your father with the whole affair and gave him instructions to go north with additional troops. He has my absolute confidence, as you know.'

Sir Josiah pulled a letter from his waistcoat pocket.

'I have a letter from him, written to you before all of this, which I now give you. He is a considerate father, is he not?'

Helen tore the letter open and read it as she walked up and down the conservatory between the gorgeous blooms. Sir Josiah felt they showed her off to great advantage. Aside from instructing her to stay in Calcutta and to be guided by Sir Josiah, the letter contained absolutely nothing which was of use to her. Her father promised to return once he had managed the difficulties in the north.

Helen, usually so resourceful, was at a loss as to how she could help John. Should she tell Sir Josiah that he was completely mistaken in trusting her father and that she knew that John Deuchars was innocent? Helen wanted to beg him to send his own sepoys without delay, yet how ridiculous it would sound? She determined, nonetheless, to try and engage Sir Josiah's help.

Sir Josiah still wondered how Helen could receive the news of her cousin's fall from grace without some form of expression – tears, or a little faint, perhaps. He looked for some feminine gesture which would enable him to give appropriate assistance. There was no entrée for him at all and he felt it was not the right moment to make any further offer of help. He would send a message later, perhaps, and conditional on her coming to him for supper when she was a little recovered. He might even venture to hold her hand again. Helen's next comments therefore took him by surprise.

She confided that she felt her father could sometimes be hasty, and had spoken to her of his authority and influence in the region. She told Sir Josiah that she felt he might perhaps be overzealous. Helen said she was concerned that, in his haste to find the culprits, he might overstep his instructions and attract more publicity than was desirable.

Sir Josiah thought this strange; a daughter should have confidence in her father, and Helen's remarks made him uneasy. He had considered sending his own sepoys to avoid any unpleasantness, but had thought Jennings the perfect solution; now he wondered. The whole thing needed to be resolved quietly in Patna. Perhaps Jennings had been getting ideas above his station. He could not have a Company man overreaching his authority. He reassured himself that this was unlikely, however, as he was acknowledged as an excellent judge of character.

It was only after Helen was in the rickshaw and on her way home that she realised that somehow she had left Sir Josiah's home without the letter. She wondered why he had not given it to her sooner. Why had it taken him a week to produce it?

Helen found Margaret in her small kitchen, which was more like an apothecary's scullery. There were pots and pestles in neat order. Green herbs hung from the ceiling. There was an all-pervading smell of camphor. She related to Margaret the position which had been so carefully described to her by Sir Josiah. Margaret pounded away on the bench, with her back to Helen, then turned, pestle in hand.

'This is not your concern,' she said. 'You must let the Company manage its own affairs. What is this business to you? If this young man has done wrong and has been found out, that is the end of the matter. Patna is a wicked place; the Company has made it so. By all accounts the opium trade is a scandal, but we cannot change everything at once. We have more work than we can manage here. I would appreciate your assistance, but instead you go out of the house without a word and visit Sir Josiah of all people! You know I personally dislike the man and you also know that he does not approve of the work we do here. Aside from all of this, he is old enough to be your father. You must be aware that there are rumours all over the town?'

Helen began to feel uncomfortable. She picked up a sheaf of newly picked herbs and pressed them to her face.

'I don't know what you mean,' she protested. 'I went to him because he said I may go to him at any time. He is kind and charming – and he has helped us, has he not, with little Esme. I wish *he* were my father rather than the one I have, who is a scoundrel and who has been sent on some wicked business which I am certain has something to do with my poor cousin. I am sorry if you do not want me to go to Sir Josiah's house. I did it to make sure John was safe, and now I know he most certainly is not.'

This was all said as Helen plucked vigorously at the wilting flowers.

Who else had she to confide in now, save Margaret? Sir Josiah, to whom she had gone for information and some kind of assistance, had completely misunderstood.

'Sir Josiah has been taken in by my father, as almost everyone is,' Helen began. She then told Margaret of her father's instruction in the letter that she should accept Sir Josiah's support and of Daniel Jennings's financial plans, which he had said made her alliance with

Sir Josiah necessary. She also alluded to her fears that John Deuchars was in danger, accused of dreadful crimes which she knew he had not the wit to commit.

Helen told Margaret that Sir Josiah must have kept the letter for some purpose, or he would have shown it to her immediately. Margaret took time to think about Helen's account of her meeting with the Major and her decision to go to Sir Josiah. With a protective arm around Helen's shoulders, she spoke softly.

'Dear Helen, I would advise you not to involve yourself in the affairs of these men. You cannot help John Deuchars. I must respect Sir Josiah's wisdom and influence in matters relating to the Company. However I may disapprove, he has huge experience in the workings of trade in this country. Even I acknowledge his authority here. We simply cannot afford to interfere. I have argued with him, to be sure, but this is quite different; this is a Company affair. As for this John Deuchars, do not imagine that you are in love with him. It is an entirely false feeling, because true and selfless love is something greater. This is infatuation and it began when you had nothing and nobody to care for you. You thought he might come to love you, but his attention may have been kindness alone. Now you have us, our little family and the work of this house.'

Helen stood up and began to protest, but Margaret was firm.

'Please, Helen, do not let us argue, for we are such friends. I did not mean that he may not have some feelings for you, for how can I know? I have not met this boy. I realise you are concerned about him, but what could you do to help him even if he is in trouble? You have your whole life's work in front of you. I have found your help so valuable and I am grateful for everything you do for me. Your companionship and your help with my work is essential to me. I have really come to depend upon you. I do think, though, that you are letting your feelings for this boy cloud a judgement upon which I have come to rely.'

Margaret put her hand under Helen's chin and raised her head so that they looked at each other. Helen noticed what a lovely face the older woman had when she did not frown.

'After all,' continued Margaret, 'what do you really know about John Deuchars? On what do you base your opinion of him? Do you really know his character? Or rather, how do you know what he is capable of? Sir Josiah is correct in that the temptations here are many. I would not presume to tell you where to place your affections. I would only say that young love may look exciting, but it seldom lasts. Let us not talk about husbands either, young or old. You may find one in time, but please let it not be either this boy or Sir Josiah.' Margaret smiled as she went on. 'Come, Helen, we will not think of this anymore.'

Helen sighed.

'I am so frightened for John,' she said. 'You can have no conception of how ruthless my father can be.'

Margaret had heard enough. She was tired and had seen a particularly young girl, no more than twelve years of age, give birth that day. There was so much to do. She waved Helen's concerns away.

'I am sure,' she said, 'that, while my race have good reason to doubt it, I feel that no man could be so wicked and cunning as to conspire in the way you say your father has done. To work for the imprisonment – or worse, the death – of an innocent young compatriot, I feel this is altogether too much. I will give you something to drink which will cool you and help you to sleep.'

Helen could tell that Margaret was now out of patience. It was only then that they noticed a considerable noise coming from the adjoining room.

'Badshah Raj!' Margaret shouted, louder than she had intended. 'The noise, man – whatever is the matter with you?'

Margaret's manservant, devotee and patient champion bowed his head and stepped through the low doorway.

'Madam, I have heard all that you have said. I would not interfere in your affairs, but your honourable brother, may he rest in peace, would not forgive me if I were to say nothing. I have heard of this man Jennings. In fact I have personal experience of him. I have said nothing to you because I thought we must respect the father of your young friend. It is she who comes to you now and it is she who is fearful. I must tell you, with many pardons, that he is a very dangerous man who hurts all who come near him. My cousin's husband is now landless when once he was a rich man. His losses were at the hand of Sahib Jennings. He raises land rents without the Company's knowledge until my cousin and others like him can no longer pay and cannot stay on their own land, and then he sells that land to grow the poppy and takes money for himself.

'Here in this town he has attempted to take money from my family but I have prevented him. He has threatened me with the magistrate. He is known to have made men disappear. He has three women and none of them are his wives, he beats them and …'

Margaret held up her hand to indicate that further detail was inappropriate. Badshah Raj nodded his understanding and continued, turning to Helen.

'He is not a good man, not at all. If this young man has something he wants, or stands in his way, Sahib Jennings will make him disappear. It is well known that he is in debt to the Chinese and that you are to be the wife of Sahib Coatsworth. Everyone says that if you do not marry Sahib Coatsworth your father will be ruined by the people to whom he owes money.'

Badshah Raj turned back to Margaret.

'Beware of Jennings. Keep out of his way, Memsahib Alexander.'

Margaret looked long at Badshah Raj, then at Helen, who was pale and said nothing.

Margaret retreated to the scullery and emerged with several canvas bags. Badshah Raj was horrified. His well-meant warning had resulted in immediate preparations to travel the 450 miles north to Patna. Margaret could tell by the way he made dispositions that he was not in good humour. He had been with her for years prior to Mr Alexander's death. He had served with her brother and had been as devoted to him; Margaret could not imagine life without him. She was teaching his sons English, and he supported her healing work. He had once expressed an opinion about her involvement with the women at the palace, but decided not to repeat the experience. Margaret, in turn, thought him indispensable and the best of men. They had absolute respect for each other's beliefs. He had a wife and three daughters, but Margaret was as much his family as they were. Neither Badshah Raj nor Margaret would have acknowledged how much they depended upon and loved each other.

His regard for her and hers for him was expressed in deeds, in his care and anxiety for her. Her reliance on his integrity and good sense was established and immutable. Their relationship transcended the normal dialogue of men and women, of culture and creed. Who is to say it cannot be so? In truth, the Missionary Society would say just that; they would say it must not be. It was as well they were thousands of miles away in Glasgow. Badshah had prepared for Margaret's return to India; he had expected it. In his mind she helped the unfortunate and the sick; she was a wonderful woman and to be preferred to those who came in search of riches. He had looked forward to Margaret's return and told everyone she was coming, but he had not expected Helen. The fact that she was Daniel Jennings's daughter had concerned him from the outset. Jennings's reputation was well known, but Badshah Raj had kept his own counsel until now. He could not permit any person to injure Margaret Alexander. Helen prompted his crossness and Margaret knew it. In the days of preparation which followed he was especially rude to Helen, the cause of this upheaval, the daughter of Sahib Jennings. Margaret wanted to make a start with as little fuss as possible. As was her custom when Badshah Raj was not pleased with her, she put him in charge of everything. In this way he was bad tempered but extremely busy.

Chapter Eleven

It would take more than two weeks to reach Patna. Badshah Raj was used to people taking his advice and was hurt that Memsahib Alexander had not. He had meant to make her see that interfering with this Jennings should not be attempted. He had tried to explain that he was too dangerous. He told her in private what he could not divulge in front of Helen: that he had known Jennings years before in the native regiment. Scandalous rumours of his working for the enemy surrounded him. None of the other officers or men had trusted him and on the fateful night of the massacre Daniel Jennings had miraculously survived. Margaret knew that her brother had died due to the incompetence of others. Badshah Raj left her in no doubt who was blamed that night and how the whole affair had been hushed up to avoid scandal in the regiment.

Now here they were, embarking on a perilous journey north, involved in an affair in which Daniel Jennings had a hand. It was dangerous work and Badshah Raj was determined that he would not let them go alone. He went about his preparations in silence. He would have continued to do so had not Helen asked him about arrangements for comfort and accommodation en route. Badshah Raj turned upon her.

'Comfort? You speak to me of comfort! Where you are going there is none. I do not approve of Memsahib Alexander putting herself in danger for you or your people. So many here need her.

You are like all your countrymen, you think only of yourselves. You all believe your concerns are more important than ours.'

Helen was taken aback.

'My goodness! You do not approve of me at all, do you? I only asked about accommodation and our stopping points. I only wanted to make sure we will travel by the most direct route.'

'I do not like or dislike you, memsahib,' Badshah Raj replied slowly, 'but what can you know about this country or safe ways to travel in it? You are a woman living in Memsahib Alexander's house in Calcutta. You can have no idea of the dangers you will encounter.'

Helen looked at him and saw he was trying to conceal his anger.

'What have I done to make you so furious with me?' she asked. 'You do not treat me as you treat Memsahib Alexander. We are both strangers here and both women, yet you treat her with the greatest respect. I can see that you dislike me and wish I had never come here. Why is that?'

'Because,' said Badshah Raj, 'she is Memsahib Alexander, sister of my trusted comrade in arms. She is the friend of the poor, and has proved herself a true friend of my family. You are the daughter of Sahib Jennings, and you have brought unnecessary trouble to her home. As to how I speak to you, I speak to you as I speak to others of your kind and country. You are here to take what you want. You have no place here, but you take as if it is your right. You are just like your countrymen who are despoiling this great country.'

Helen was shaken.

'Badshah Raj, we have helped Margaret together, worked at the clinic. I cared for Claire when she was so ill. I thought I had been helpful to Margaret and that you and your family accepted me.'

'What do you know about trust, memsahib? To be trusted is not something you can demand of another person. Trust cannot be created just because you will it. It can take a lifetime to trust another soul, and moments to destroy that trust. You must also know that I have never asked you to call me Badshah Raj. You have taken it upon yourself to call me by that name because you have heard others do so and because you think it is your right. You have assumed you could address me in the same way as people who are my family and my friends. I am a prince – is this how you address princes in your country? You have no respect for me, my family or this place.'

'Well,' said Helen, 'then you must tell me what I must properly call you. If I have given any offence, I apologise for it.'

Badshah Raj looked directly at her.

'In fact, memsahib, women of my house do not address me directly, and wait for me to speak to them.'

Helen was indignant.

'Margaret Alexander does not wait for any man to address her – she speaks her mind. And I mean to do likewise.'

Badshah Raj smiled; she seemed to have spirit, this girl. Perhaps she was not her father's daughter, after all. He paused before speaking again.

'I have known Memsahib Alexander many years and her husband too. I have reason to thank her and to trust her. Memsahib Alexander is a teacher; she teaches my sons what they will need to know in order to outwit men like your father and the rapacious men who come after him.'

'So,' said Helen, 'you see me as my father. We are one and the same as far as you are concerned. You dislike everything about me and wish I was out of this house?'

'I say again, I neither like nor dislike you,' said Badshah Raj. 'I seek neither to please or to displease you. You are the friend of Memsahib Alexander, she who is a friend to all. I respect her for her knowledge and her goodness. I must respect your father, but I do this in the same way that I would respect a cobra – because of his reputation. I would be foolish not to be respectful of the cobra.'

'And so, in your mind,' said Helen, 'I am the daughter of the cobra?'

Badshah Raj bowed, turned his back and left the room.

They had debated whether to attempt the journey by land or by river. Badshah Raj regarded any such travel as unwise. He had been afforded little preparation time, but he had enlisted his two powerfully built nephews to accompany them. In addition, they took three scouts and five servants. They were not a large party but they were well armed and well equipped. Badshah Raj had forgotten little since his time with the Bengal Native Infantry. They would stay in villages en route each night for safety.

The first day's journey took them past flat marshlands which had been partially drained, but the insects would trouble them; flies rose from the marshes in black clouds. Margaret had prepared a thick lotion which they smeared in foul-smelling layers on their arms and necks. It was surprisingly effective, and only Helen was badly bitten.

Margaret tried to comfort her by saying that once they left the marshes things would improve, and as the outskirts of Calcutta disappeared behind them, the landscape began to change. The flat land with its unending paddy fields gradually gave way to scrub. There were settlements at intervals along the route. The reception in the first village was warm and hospitable. They were glad of the shelter and comfort which proximity to the villagers gave. Sleeping arrangements were comfortable and water was fetched before breakfast in the cool of the morning. Helen observed a way of life of which she had been previously unaware. People in the villages had their own routines and customs, unfettered by the requirements of the city. Here it seemed people were not constrained; they lived their own lives. On hearing her make this observation, Badshah Raj quietly shook his head.

After several days they stopped in mid-afternoon at Guptipara to see the nearby terracotta Vaishnava Temples – four shrines dedicated to Chaitanya, Brindabanchandra, Ramchandra and Krishnachandra – but they were not permitted to enter. Badshah Raj looked over at Margaret Alexander and smiled. It all looked so ancient and breathtakingly beautiful, with panels showing gods watching the battle of Lanka, and the Banar sena (army of monkeys).

Helen had marvelled at the sights and sounds of the city, but the countryside was different. The land was beautiful. They seemed to be stopping continually because Badshah Raj and his family were well known and welcome. He seemed to feel it was imperative to stop at every bend in the river to accept hospitality; consequently, their progress was slow. Helen's spirits settled as the days passed. In the early morning when it was cool, she listened to the call of the black-hooded oriole. She laughed at the antics of small grey macaques in the trees, who chattered loudly as they passed.

At the end of the first week's travel, on a particularly starlit night she sat outside. Wrapping her *dolai* closely around her, she felt curiously peaceful. She had her back to the *ghur*, which had been lit to keep away animals. The vast and darkening sky was set with a million burning stars. They did not twinkle like stars at home but shone so brightly that it hurt her eyes to look at them. Helen could make out Cassiopeia, and Pegasus, the winged horse. She listened in the stillness, watching the now thin pink glow diminish on the horizon. The only sounds beyond the village were the pond herons and the cinnamon bitterns who called in the last of the twilight. Later when darkness fell, the last sound Helen heard was the nightjar, the bringer of sleep, crying in the distance.

Calcutta and the coast were left far behind. Helen was glad to be travelling towards John, but more than that she was enjoying the journey. Badshah Raj and she were not speaking to each other directly, but Helen was content. There was general agreement to travel with the Hooghly and camp before noon on the shore to avoid the searing heat of day. They then set off again, travelling into the evening and stopping at nightfall. Night travel carried its own particular risks, but the midday heat was so unforgiving that this compromise was necessary. The Hooghly was a wide river, navigable by ocean-going ships for thirty miles from Calcutta. Even so, care was needed in the management of their little boats.

This wild country was predominantly grass-covered, interspersed with forest and low trees. At night they tried to avoid the heavily wooded areas. Even Badshah Raj was cautious, and someone was always posted on watch for predators, whether human or animal.

The party was increased before they arrived at the low hills with guides who accompanied them to deter thieves. Badshah Raj advised caution until the rice beer the guides brought with them had been consumed. Helen decided they looked so fierce that she would not speak to them at all. Margaret seemed to be at ease with them and Helen marvelled, not for the first time, at the Scot's knowledge of the local dialect.

The villages were without exception welcoming. The simple accommodation offered was preferable to sleeping outside. Meals were wholesome; the villagers had access to small game but their diet was cooked pulses made into little cakes, rice boiled up with sugar, or a mix of wild potatoes and flour. Everything seemed to be fried in a watery butter. There was always rice, and something called *gatta* which was cloyingly sweet and which Badshah Raj's nephews ate greedily and then picked from between their teeth. Helen tried not to watch.

Margaret was very particular about the water. However deliciously cool the streams looked, she insisted on boiling all before she or Helen touched it. This caused great amusement and much shaking of heads. Washing was rudimentary and hardly adequate. Helen learned to bite the end of a sprig of wood until the frayed fibres were softened to make an effective toothbrush. She also learned the hard way that it was essential to shake out her *sitalpati* before lying down on it. Insects and other creatures nestled uninvited in its folds, which, if not removed, made for an uncomfortable night. The journey was physically demanding and Helen found that, despite the age difference between them, Margaret generally appeared to manage as well as she did.

Helen was at last obliged to accept help from Badshah Raj's nephews. She gradually became accustomed to the travelling and to the camp routine. Helen wondered if John had taken time to draw on his journey north.

One day the party stopped early and went ashore close to another shrine. Helen asked Badshah Raj if it was absolutely essential that they should stop again, as it was hours to nightfall. He simply nodded towards Margaret Alexander, who was resting against a stone wall. He had noticed that Margaret was tiring. Helen had been keen to travel as quickly as possible and had already spoken to Margaret about the number of times they had stopped to pay respects, to pray or to accept hospitality. Margaret had only said that Badshah Raj knew what he was doing; she would not interfere in his organisation and Helen must accept his knowledge of what was safe and appropriate. She felt guilty now that she had harangued Margaret about the number of times they had rested. Palm trees hung over the shrine giving some shade and Helen threw down a *sitalpati* from her bed bundle and lay down. Margaret also made good use of the opportunity once she had rested, minutely examining the inscriptions on nearby rocks. She was gently admonished by Badshah Raj for straying too far from the group. Margaret would not have tolerated such a comment from any other living soul.

Helen lay on the parched grass waiting for the men to emerge from the shrine. It was hot and she was sleepy. She half-opened her eyes and became aware of a large shadow which obscured the sun. Badshah Raj loomed over her; he had Margaret at his side. His deep voice lowered in an effort to whisper.

'*Suti Khar tar sapanai dharhar.*'

It seemed to echo through the ruins of the shrine. Helen lay dreaming of the Vaishnava temples. She was walking among the characters on the walls as the dust rose from their feet. She imagined the interior walls of the temples covered in gorgeous plants and succulent fruit. Stepping towards a lemon tree covered in blossom, she stroked the dripping leaves. Helen watched as the branches began to fasten around her hands. The lemon tree's flowers were wonderfully fragrant at first but the smell intensified and she was sickened. She pulled at the tendrils, trying to wrench free. She began to panic, but then heard a voice and it was comforting. The bindings on her hands seemed to loosen. Helen opened her eyes and sat up slowly.

'What did he say? Where am I?'

Margaret smiled and turned to Badshah Raj.

'He only said "she sleeps on grass and dreams of palaces",' she said to Helen reassuringly.

Helen scrambled to her feet, a little shakily, perspiration standing on her forehead.

'I would certainly exchange my lot at this moment for the hot water comforts of a palace,' she said.

Margaret thought not.

Two days after they joined the Ganges from the Hooghly, the boat passed through a ravine near Pirpainti, where the river bends around the Rajmahal Hills. The party was tired and quiet, and there was a tension which Helen could not explain. She reasoned it was just fatigue and the effects of the journey. Margaret moved carefully in the boat. She had brought Helen water and, when handing the bottle to her, kissed her reassuringly on the cheek for no apparent reason. There seemed to be something not quite as it should be – everyone felt it. The river and the birdsong were as beautiful as ever, there was no reason for anxiety – and yet they all fell silent.

Badshah Raj wanted to continue beyond the shale path which ran beside the river. He signalled to pull the boats up in a more secure place. It was mid-morning but the air was still and unbearably hot, trapped by the towering jet-black rocks which appeared to glisten in the sunlight. The decision to stop would have to be made soon, as they had been travelling since dawn. Suddenly, the boy in the lead vessel shouted and gestured ahead. Kites were slowly circling above the river bank. There was something on the shoreline, half-concealed by the overhang. This was not usually significant, as animals were frequently killed at the water's edge and their rotting remains attracted all manner of predators.

This was a dangerous stretch of the river and Badshah Raj, ever cautious of banditry, moved close to protect the women. There was a hurried discussion between Badshah Raj and his nephews. The lead boat drew closer to the bank. Badshah Raj's nephews called out, their voices echoing against the rock walls. All the boats moved slowly to shore; there was a collective nervousness. The river lay deep between the rocks and there would be no escape if someone came at them here. It would be an ideal place to trap and rob unsuspecting travellers. They knew that not all people in that area were friendly.

Margaret called to Badshah Raj, who had also seen something crouched against the rock face. It could still be a trap, but they were committed now. The boats pushed towards the shore. Helen felt cold and, unaccountably, she began to shake. Badshah Raj's nephews had primed their guns and she was pushed unceremoniously into the back of the boat. As the men jumped to shore Badshah Raj, seeing Margaret about to do the same, held her back.

The crumpled, bloody remains of a man lay on the shingle. It looked as if he had crawled halfway under the rock to get out of the sun. Who could survive in full sun and in this heat? Margaret pushed Badshah Raj aside – she had seen a small movement. The man was cut to ribbons, but he was alive. He was in European dress and lying on his front. The clothing on his shoulders was torn away, revealing flesh which fell down his back in ribbons. He appeared to have been scarified by something sharp, his clothing and the flesh cut in neat striations.

Helen had emerged, unseen by the others. She saw his torso; it looked as though it had been gouged by hundreds of claws. With help from Badshah Raj, Margaret turned the man carefully onto his side. He had a deep wound under his ribcage and broken ribs had pierced the flesh. Whatever had been used had also lacerated the tops of his legs. His face was swollen, his eyes blackened. Yellow matter oozed from where his eyes ought to have been. His flesh was rent from his cheeks, as it appeared that the same tool had torn at his face. He had lost a lot of blood and was, mercifully, deeply unconscious. He looked quite young, as far as it was possible to tell, but painfully thin. Margaret had him carried under some nearby trees and set up shade and shelter around him. She could do little for his wounds, which were infected, but she made him as comfortable as possible. Badshah

Raj knew that these injuries were not the result of attack by animals. He was on the alert, and posted his young guards.

The injured man stirred as evening fell. Margaret spoke softly to him and tended him where he lay. She could do nothing as he began to shake violently, and he could not be moved again. His sand-coloured hair was caked with blood and with pieces of his scalp. He was in pain and began to moan. Margaret did not leave him as he whimpered through torn lips; he was barely audible. Margaret administered laudanum, but any attempt she made to examine his wounds or move his clothing resulted in him crying out. It was then that Badshah Raj noticed a cord around his waist. It was made of thin strips of bright material that looked as if it had been roughly torn and knotted together. The cord was fastened tightly to his thigh and from this makeshift belt hung a small pouch. The whole contraption was carefully removed.

Inside the pouch were two tiny pocketbooks. The first was the smaller, its pages neatly lined, each set out in columns and covered in tiny handwriting. It was filled with numbers and letters which could be clearly seen, although the words were difficult to make out without a glass. The second contained drawings of buildings set out in plan and, winding around them, a river. The artist had even included boats with tiny, coloured sails. It was all done in miniature, with trees and even animals in the foreground. A little hand-drawn map had been folded neatly into the back of the book. It was clear that the artist was competent. The second of the books also contained names and dates, but the pages at the back seemed to be stuck together. Helen prised off the brown paper top layer to reveal a wax pad inside. The only other item found with the man was a quantity of what looked like tea. Margaret, when shown these items, frowned and shook her head.

Badshah Raj made it clear that he would not wish to stay in the ravine overnight; whoever had attacked this man might return. However, Margaret refused to move. She gestured to Badshah Raj and walked away from where the young man lay. They spoke quietly together.

'This man has been grievously wounded,' said Margaret. 'I do not think he can be expected to live, but there is something more. He is, I fear, addicted to opium. He has certain symptoms which, notwithstanding his facial and head wounds, indicate he uses the stuff.' She opened her hand. 'I have found these powdered leaves which can be ground small and smoked. There are also the remains of a lump. Look at his teeth and his hands.'

Helen was terrified and could hardly breathe. She looked again at the bloody form. He was the same height and size as John Deuchars. Could this be him – half-dead, beaten, scratched and mortally wounded?

The man stirred, aroused by the approach of Badshah Raj's nephews. His mouth worked violently. Margaret ran to him and bent down so that her face was close to his. Helen heard her softly whispering and then she heard it.

'The Lord is my shepherd; I shall not want. He maketh me to lie down in green pastures …'

At last Margaret drew away from the shaking man and turned to the others, obviously moved.

'He is English,' she said, looking at Helen. 'Is this your John Deuchars? I want you to look at him carefully.'

Helen flinched, and Margaret reached for her hand.

'I know it is hard because he is very badly wounded.'

Helen turned, gripping Margaret, and steeled herself to look at the torn face. She heard Margaret telling her that she must go closer in order to be sure because she did not think he could last the night.

Helen could hardly bear it, but stooped to kneel beside the man. She felt Badshah Raj supporting her and was thankful for his arm. She was appalled by, and completely unprepared for, the dreadful smell. His head, stripped of flesh, was hideous. His eyes were missing and flies clustered around his broken throat. Helen felt ill. The face told her nothing, and she looked away. She made herself look again at the hands and the small, stubby fingers. Her stomach lurched in a combination of relief and shock. She knew that these were not John Deuchars' long-fingered hands. She was overwhelmed by a guilty sense of relief. Shaking her head, she heard herself say, 'It is not him. But if not John, then who?' She got to her feet and was helped to some bushes at the side of the ravine, where she vomited.

As night fell, the man's breathing became shallow. They remained on a long grass bank some distance from the water's edge, the cliffs of the ravine above them. The small camp was very still and subdued. Fires had been lit and a small meal of cakes and lentils eaten. Helen had slept all through the heat of the afternoon, and found she was surprisingly hungry. When she had awoken she could see nothing apart from the reassuring glow of the camp fire and heard only the low voices of the men. She did not sleep again. Badshah Raj and his nephews took turns to keep watch. Margaret remained with the man, who now breathed in short, rasping breaths. He moved and cried out in pain, his eye sockets opening empty, black and bloodied. He cried out, and when Margaret's hands came within reach grabbed at her. She had administered almost all the opium she carried.

Just before dawn he became very agitated but was more lucid. In a pain-filled voice full he turned towards Margaret.

'I need to tell you … who I am,' he winced. 'My name is James … James Jackson. I have done things …' and he began to sob.

The effort of speaking made his wounds ooze. The slightest noise attracted Badshah Raj, who was at Margaret's side in a moment.

'I did not want to hurt anyone,' James Jackson continued. 'They left me here … did not need me anymore. I had to do things … had to get away. I had to … no choice, you see this.'

Margaret held back his hand as he weakly raised it, searching for his face. He moved his head painfully from side to side, as if looking for light where none could be found.

'They have taken everything … all the money and the cakes. Fire, it was on fire! They shouldn't have destroyed everything. There was to be no killing. I ordered no killing.' He started to tremble and his voice became shrill. 'I could not stop them … they were madmen!'

He shook convulsively, and Margaret gently raised his head up, placing the final drop in the vial to his mouth. The last of the brown liquid against his lips, he gulped greedily, and she had to prise his hands away. He held her fast with an unnatural strength but then coughed up black gobbets of dark blood and sank back against the makeshift pillow.

It was about half an hour later that he spoke again.

'I must tell you about the factory.'

Margaret soothed him and told him to rest, but the laudanum was having some effect and he would not be quiet. He tried to pull her face closer to his.

'I arrived with the dacoits under cover of darkness,' he began, managing little more than a whisper. 'Mr Mowbray said that, if challenged, I was to say that I was someone called John Deuchars … and that we were taking half of the goods out that night. It was not unusual for Mr Mowbray to order that a consignment should leave the godowns early. He said he did it to flush out thieves. When I came here I was told the early transports carried bags of earth … but then I found out this was not the case. I told Mr Mowbray we were being robbed but he laughed at me and said I was an idiot. I was told to keep my mouth shut or I would be dismissed.

'I have never overseen as much opium as on that night. They took nearly everything … I had no choice, do you see? Mr Mowbray said Deuchars was a lazy aristocrat who was going to take his job and my medicine. … He said that everything would change unless he was dealt with. Mowbray said that once Deuchars was in prison everything would be alright … and I could go home with money and enough medicine to make me well again. I was desperate because for three nights there had been a bright moon.'

He moaned, and Margaret placed the empty phial to his lips, and he licked at it.

'I have been so ill – such dreadful shaking. Mr Mowbray gave me medicine, but it hasn't made me well. I knew the shipment date was near and that Mr Mowbray would send me home without my medicine unless I succeeded. Once the guards and the merchants arrived for the main transport, there would be no chance of taking the goods …'

After an interval to draw breath he carried on.

'Why we were to take more than was usual I don't know. Mr Mowbray was usually so careful to avoid arousing suspicion. I was to escort my men into the factory, just as I used to do when Mr Mowbray was overseeing things last time. I wore a turban and a scarf which covered my face so that the guards couldn't see who I was. I was to tell them we were making secret arrangements for transportation. Mr Mowbray said that the merchants wanted the goods removed to a secret location where attack by dacoits was less likely. They are used to sahibs telling them what to do, and they knew there were problems with security. I told them that, unless they let us pass, they would be whipped, and worse. We could see the stacks of opium ready for transport.'

He sobbed and began to bleed from his sightless eyes. His voice was weakening.

'It was not part of my orders to kill the guards. It all went wrong. Mr Mowbray said I would get my money and I could go back to England to get well. The men overpowered the guards … I tried to stop them from killing, but they went mad. All the guards posted on the river had already been killed while we were in the factory … there was no help to be had. Once the opium was in the boats, they even killed my servant. I don't know why they did not kill me. I suppose I was supposed to be this Deuchars and he had to escape. When I protested they bound me and threw me in one of the boats. I woke up in a hut of some kind. I knew the opium was gone. I don't know how long I was in the dark, but I think it was several days. I was given a very little food once a day, usually in the evening. I lost track of time. I was beaten the first time I managed to get free … I was caught trying to get to the river, and they did this.'

He felt for his face, shaking convulsively. The horror of the memory contorted the skin which was stretched tight with infection.

'They came at me with knives, stabbing me about the head. I don't remember much after that … I think they put me back in the dark in the village, because I could hear voices. They hoped I would die, but I did not. Then they brought me to the water and left me to drown. I crawled under here, where it was cooler.' His hand moved to his face again. 'I don't know why they did not kill me,' he moaned. 'Tell my mother I am coming home … I will make it right. Do not tell her you found me like this. Do not tell her that I am …' and he trailed off in a rasping sob.

The wound under his ribs bubbled ominously, blood soaking the makeshift bandages.

'Tell Mr Mowbray I want to go home now … Tell him I don't want the money, just my medicine. Tell my mother I love her and I will see her soon …'

Morning came; it was cool and bright, but James Jackson was dead. Standing beside the rock wall in the early morning, Helen watched the sun rise over the Ganges. The earth was covered in dew; a large spider's web hung from the rocks, adorned with tiny droplets like beads. They shone red in the sunlight like droplets of blood, and the whole earth glowed. The animals and birds called and chattered, and the earth seemed so full of teaming life.

The Ganges ran swiftly, swollen with mountain rain, and in the dawn sunlight its waters looked like a river of blood. The reflection of the morning sunlight was like a path leading far out into the middle of the river. Helen rehearsed her poem, the poem she had given to John: *Throw me into the streaming sun, that shining river of sea. Throw me in on a clear day, cast me away and see. Look how I sparkle on top of the waves, I am part of the thundering roar, think of me* … She broke off as a tear trickled down her cheek and she thought of the young body they had just gathered up.

They had burned him, to Margaret Alexander's disgust, near the water's edge. Badshah Raj had insisted, saying that if they buried him animals would dig him up. He had already been hacked to pieces, and should be protected from further insult, no matter what he had done.

As the sun grew hotter Helen felt dizzy. It had been a long night and she had not slept. Suddenly she felt very tired. The sun on the cool water beckoned, and Helen moved slowly to the water's edge. The slightest of breezes seemed to pluck at her hair. The golden pathway out on to the water looked so inviting. She stepped forward. An arm caught her and pulled her back – it was Margaret, and her voice was impatient.

'Helen, girl, what are you doing? Do not stand so close to the edge, woman! Your feet are wet. What are you thinking of? There are crocodiles here!'

Margaret had a too firm hold on her arm, and her voice cracked with tiredness, but Helen also heard something else. Margaret was angry.

'I need you to help me. Listen to me carefully – we have a great deal to do. If I am correct, we have to leave now. John Deuchars may have very little time left.'

Margaret let go of Helen's arm and looked closely at her, frowning. She kept forgetting just how young and inexperienced Helen was. Margaret gently put her arm around her shoulders. Helen made no sound and yet the tears ran down her face. The older woman just held her, and they stood together, leaning one on the other.

'He was so young, and so ill,' whispered Helen. 'He was younger than John and all he wanted to do was to go home instead of being halfway across the world. He called for his mother. What must it be like to feel so alone?'

Margaret sighed and turned to Helen.

'Remember, the scriptures say that we are only in this world as travellers. We go through this life to another and a better country.

Travel we must, all of us in our own way. We are never alone in dealing with whatever crosses our path, good or evil. It is true that some people meet with evil and are unprepared, and that is cruel. We did what we could for this young man – we did what his mother would have wished, and we will do more for him if we confront those who brought him to this.' She shuddered as she pointed to the heap of ash near the water's edge. 'Come, Helen, we must hurry if you would help John Deuchars.'

'Margaret, I know that you think me a stupid fool. At least I am not some vain girl in search of a rich man. I don't want to trap him. I just want him to see what we could be to each other.'

'Oh, Helen, this will not do – it won't do at all. Love should be something a man and a woman feel together. It requires two devoted people. You have said nothing to me which makes me think this John Deuchars thinks the same of you. Are you absolutely sure that he does? You deserve more – you deserve a man who would travel around the world in search of you. I gave my heart to a man who could only love his God. Do not imagine feeling useful is any substitute for loving. Please do not follow in my footsteps!'

The party reached Patna as dusk was falling on a sultry evening with the burning red sun on their faces. The town was quiet, and they were exhausted. Badshah Raj's nephew had gone ashore and ridden ahead to the outskirts to secure accommodation for them.

Margaret was determined to find Daniel Jennings without delay. On making enquiry they were advised that he was up-country in conference with his Chinese contacts, trying to salvage part of the opium order.

The following day, late in the evening, the door to their bungalow flew open and Jennings appeared in the living room. Margaret was reading one of the small notebooks. Helen was by then sleeping soundly and Badshah Raj was out looking for supplies.

Jennings was furious and demanded an explanation.

'For what reason and by whose authority do you come here through dangerous country and alone? Are you all mad?'

Margaret looked directly at him.

'Mr Jennings, I came here with particular purpose and I am not alone.'

'You are as good as alone, madam, as you have no Englishman with you. Do you think it is safe and right that you should wander around Bengal Presidency with your male servants?'

'Mr Jennings, I am safe in the Lord's hands,' Margaret replied. 'As to what is proper, I think it may be assumed I am at the age where a woman is in no danger of that kind. I am here by right; there is nothing to say that I might not go as I please in Bengal Presidency as an emissary of Galen, or the Lord, for that matter. In this particular case I have come with purpose to save a man's life. I met with a poor wretch on the way who, though cut to the bone and half-dead, was able to tell me who he was and something of his history.'

'Madam, I will find out what the blazes you are doing here. Then I will see to it that you go back whence you came. I will not listen to your holier-than-thou account of saving some native on the road. I have at this time most pressing difficulties with regard to trade. As if that were not enough, I have a Company prisoner under lock and key – an Englishman, if you can believe it!'

Margaret remained calm.

'Mr Jennings, before I speak to you about the young man you have detained, I must tell you that accompanying me on this journey is your daughter, Helen.'

Jennings stared at her, and ran his hand through his hair. He was not a reasonable man. He made no pretence about it. Daniel Jennings had not achieved anything in life by being reasonable. He had found that a practised impatience worked to great effect and, where that failed, incandescent rage achieved more than polite reason.

Compounding his already short temper was absence of sleep. He hurled a chair in Margaret's direction, but she did not flinch.

'Helen would come because she is sure that you have the wrong man in relation to this, and now I agree with her. I must say that encouragement of trade in narcotics is a dreadful business. Do not think that I have not heard of it – it breeds sin and misery, but I am not here to discuss that. I know that there has been a robbery and a fire, has there not? I now believe you have the idea that John Deuchars has committed crime. You must release him immediately.'

'Madam, what can you know of any robbery, and what were you thinking of to have brought my daughter to this place?'

He was enraged by the disasters which seemed to compound by the hour. Angry and unguarded, he moved towards Margaret.

'You are an interfering old woman, a meddling old hag! What gives you the right to lecture me, witch? I have to accommodate a secretary of trade who knows nothing of the realities of life out here. I do not have to listen to you; in fact, I hate women like you. You should be locked up! I could make you disappear and nobody would ask any questions. I could lift my finger and you would be gone!'

He was shouting now, his face livid as he raged at her.

'You come here to convert people you know nothing about. They do not need you – they have their own gods. Oh no, meddle, meddle, you come just the same with your self- righteous nonsense. Now you have brought my daughter many miles through rough country with a band of savages and you call yourself a woman of God! You are a self-serving hypocrite! You and your kind are a plague on India.'

In response, Margaret's voice was as quiet and calm as his was loud.

'I follow my conscience, Mr Jennings. I live as I feel the Lord would wish me to. It is my calling. You can insult me, but there is nothing you can say which has not already been said. I spread the Gospel of Jesus Christ and I make no apology for it. I offer no apology for your daughter's presence. She is attached to this young man John Deuchars, and she would come. I have warned her against this. I have heard you prefer Sir Josiah, but I hardly think your choice for her is better. However, this is not what I wish to speak to you about. I will ignore your temper and your rudeness because there are other pressing and important maters which take precedence.

'I wanted to see you urgently, and you must hear me out and then you will leave. Please, if you can manage it, be calm or I will call for aid and make you listen. I must tell you of events which have relevance to the robbery at Patna.'

Margaret calmly told Jennings about the young man on the riverside and the proofs she had found. When he asked to see the small brown notebooks, she showed him one but would not give it up. Margaret advised him that the others were in safe keeping. She did not trust him. Jennings was absolutely clear that he must have the notebooks as proof positive.

'You do not think well of me, either as a man or as a father,' he said, turning at the door. 'Think what you will on that score. I have a strong case against John Deuchars and I will take some persuading to give it up. I have listened to you, but I am not wholly convinced. You will not provide the proof you speak of, and ask me to accept your word. You say that you found this man on the road and you show me a book full of scrawl. I do not think that is worth very much. I do not think a great deal of your worth, either. You have interfered where you are not wanted, but then that is your whole career, is it not? You know nothing about the needs of this country or its people. Do not imagine we encourage the trade here, for it needs none. The Chinese cannot get enough of the poppy and the farmers here are keen enough to grow it. We merely coordinate and administer the movement of the goods and I will not tolerate your interference. I do not consider my daughter as knowing her own mind, but henceforth I mean to make sure she is guided by me as to the wisest course. She will return to Calcutta without delay. Now hand her over to me, if you please – she can hardly have slept through our discussions.'

'I think,' said Margaret slowly, 'that you are misguided. Come now, we have been quite frank enough with one another for one evening. Your daughter appears to me to know her own mind and will stay with me for the present. You seem to be more out of sorts than is safe. In fact, I would not entrust her to you. As to your role in the selling of opium, you make no headway with me. Your long exposure to these vices has blinded you to right thinking. All I am asking you to do in the case of John Deuchars is to make a further enquiry based on information I have given to you. That is all I have to say, except that if you fail to make appropriate arrangements and any harm comes to John Deuchars I will take all the evidence I have to Sir Josiah without delay. We will see what he thinks about your management of this affair.'

Jennings looked at her with loathing.

'I will make the enquiries I see fit, and I will act as I choose!'

'And so will I!' replied Margaret.

Jennings moved towards her, close enough that she could smell his breath.

'I propose that you try to convince His Majesty's Government about the detrimental effect on the Chinese of the opium trade – see how far it gets you. Begin on your return to Calcutta with His Excellency; I would pay to see that!'

He was mocking her, knowing that the British government more than condoned the trade in opium – it relied upon it. He gripped her arm too tightly.

'Now hand over my daughter, before I really lose my temper!'

A large figure appeared silhouetted against the dimness.

'I have just returned,' interjected Badshah Raj. 'Are you in need of me, Memsahib Alexander?'

Jennings let go of Margaret's arm and stepped away. She was glad to see Badshah Raj, who now moved towards her protectively. She placed her hand on Badshah Raj's arm to steady herself; he understood, allowing this strong woman to lean on him only for a moment.

Margaret held on to Badshah Raj but continued to look directly at Jennings.

'All is well, Badshah Raj. I am guided and safe by the grace of God.'

Jennings looked from one to the other and smiled unpleasantly. 'Ah, so *this* is how it is,' he said.

Badshah Raj stepped towards Jennings, but before he could get hold of him another figure appeared. Helen and her father stared at each other for a moment, and then Jennings barked at her to get dressed. Instead, Helen moved slowly towards Badshah Raj. Jennings made a grab for her, but she pulled free and ran towards Margaret. Helen stared at her father.

'I am not leaving with you unless you agree to take me to release John.'

Jennings looked scornfully at the three of them and laughed.

'You expect me to listen to this old woman! You want me to take you to Deuchars and then release him! You are all quite mad. I will do no such thing. The man is guilty and he will hang.'

Helen threw herself at her father.

'Take me to my John!' she screamed. 'Take me to him! You are a monster! I hate you!'

She fell weeping at his feet and lay sobbing on the floor. There was no point in Jennings remaining, and he looked down at Helen.

'I will see you in the morning, when I hope you will be more rational. Do not forget that I am your father and I require you to come with me. Old woman, you should go home. They burned the likes of you in times past. Beware, they still burn women here. I expect whatever evidence you have to be given to me tomorrow without fail, all of it – do you understand?'

Jennings was appalled that his daughter was weak – obviously not as much like him as he had thought. He turned and made for the door, closely followed by Badshah Raj. In the darkness he felt a hand behind him and was propelled into the night air, landing on his knees in the dusty road. The door of the house slammed behind him. Jennings jumped furiously to his feet. Badshah Raj would pay for that! Inside the house, Margaret Alexander put her arms around Helen and suddenly felt very tired indeed.

Chapter Twelve

Jennings made up his mind to settle his score with Badshah Raj and his wretched family. He had ways of managing these things. Jennings did not like surprises – he needed to remain in control. This talk of the stranger found on the side of the river was inconvenient. He wished Shuja were with him, but he was somewhere in the hills, negotiating with the Chinese. Jennings could not afterwards remember what prompted him to make his way to see that his prisoner was still safe under lock and key. Something made him think that the old woman and her man might try to spirit Deuchars away.

He would not allow it. His traders were gone, the remaining goods were ruined and he was unpaid, which meant he could not settle what he owed in Calcutta. He considered how he was to ensure that Helen did what she was told. Her marriage to Sir Josiah was imperative – nobody could touch him as the father of her ladyship. He had been too accommodating but he would know how to manage now. He was always at his best in a real crisis. She had run wild since he left England, but she would feel again the discipline of her youth. He would knock out the rubbish that woman had put into her head. Once he was Sir Josiah Coatsworth's son-in-law he would make sure the Alexander woman was sent packing. The nerve of that bitch – how dare she deny him access to his own daughter? She had meddled in Company affairs and withheld evidence. By God, he would have her thrown out of India.

He thought on this and his fury rose again. He would move John Deuchars to a more secure place just in case the Alexander woman tried to release him. Nobody got the better of Daniel Jennings. As he approached the low bungalow he noticed that the guards were not outside the building; torchlights burned in every window. He quickened his step and rapped on the door. It was not locked and swung open on its hinges. Guards were standing at either side of the door to the rear strong room, but they were guards he did not recognise. Their huge forms were shielding the low bed on which John Deuchars lay. A woman was leaning over the bed and stroking Deuchars' head while speaking softly. She had long, thin white fingers, on one of which sat the most enormous ring, glowing ruby-red. He could not see her face but a blonde plait as thick as a man's hand coiled down her back. She did not turn, but a beautiful voice said, 'Good evening, Mr Jennings'.

Drifting in and out of consciousness, John found, in place of rough handling, an angel leaning over him. She turned and gently bathed his parched lips. John's limbs felt as though he was on fire – this was death and joy intermingled. Julia Coatsworth had no regrets about her decision to travel with sixteen of Sir Josiah's sepoys but, looking at John, she felt she was too late. She had encouraged her father's nagging doubts about the trouble in Patna and when he agreed troops should be sent north she had left with them, unseen among the servants and water-carriers. Her dress and knowledge of the language ensured that she was not detected. She had only made herself known to the commanding officer when it was too late to send her back to Calcutta. After this she had travelled quite comfortably. There would be trouble when she returned home, but she would worry about that later.

Julia had found John's mattress lying in water in a fetid cell. Rancid food was strewn on a filthy floor of bare earth. She had removed from him the small earthenware bowl over which he was running a fevered finger.

'Each chest, forty balls, seers and chittaks, all spoiled,' he moaned.

John's feet were crudely bandaged with pieces of his shirt. No other attempt had been made to attend to his wounds. Julia could see that the blood and infection had soaked through his clothes. He was very hot; perspiration was running down his brow. Julia doubted he could be moved safely, but she needed to get him out of this disgusting guardroom. Any attempt to transport him to medical help was dangerous; he would not survive the journey. It had not been part of her plan to rescue her future husband, only to have him die in her arms.

John was barely conscious but he kept trying to speak, slurring his words. He repeated, over and over, 'perfect flower, perfect flower'. Julia was just about to order a sepoy to lift John from his filthy makeshift bed when Daniel Jennings arrived.

'Is every damn woman in Calcutta come to Patna?' he roared. 'Margaret Alexander, my daughter, now you!'

Julia turned quickly and her heart leapt, realising immediately that John had a chance. If Margaret Alexander was in Patna, John could be saved. She turned to Jennings.

'Are you telling me that Margaret Alexander is here? Then go and get her immediately.'

'I certainly will not! You are in my jurisdiction and this is my prisoner.'

Julia turned her cool blue eyes on him.

'Get her, Jennings, or I will not answer for my actions when I return to Calcutta. I mean this man to live. You choose what kind of report concerning your conduct reaches my father. I would suggest you do exactly as I ask.'

She turned and tenderly stroked John's head. His eyes fluttered open and he appeared to look directly at her. She bent forward, kissed his forehead and murmured, 'Darling'.

Daniel Jennings was not slow on the uptake. If Julia was here, then her father would not be far away. Whatever the circumstances, he knew this was not the time to argue. If Sir Josiah Coatsworth had plans for Deuchars he would not interfere, even if Deuchars was a rogue. Jennings would not cross Sir Josiah or his daughter. He smiled and bowed.

'I shall get Margaret Alexander immediately – much good it will do.'

It was three in the morning and the dawn was breaking as Margaret, under escort, reached John Deuchars. She knew at once that his life hung in the balance.

When Helen awoke the sun was shining brightly and she realised it was late. She had turned the events of the previous evening over in her mind until the early hours, when she had finally slept. The house appeared to be completely empty and quiet. She started up and frantically grabbed her clothes. She was desperate to go to John, but where was he? She had no idea where to look. Then she thought Badshah Raj's nephews would know where he was being held. She dressed and rushed through the house, only to be told that Margaret had been called away long before dawn and Badshah Raj had gone with her. They did not know where John was and insisted repeatedly that they had instructions to remain with her in the bungalow. She was furious with them for their blind obedience to Badshah Raj and with Margaret for leaving without her. Helen impatiently paced the dark hallway, then collected her things and set out alone. Making her way through the trees towards the road, she saw Margaret. Helen rushed towards her, but something in Margaret's face brought her up sharply.

Margaret was weary, and drew her cloak about her closed her eyes for a moment before speaking.

'Helen, my dear girl, there is something you must know. We have found John Deuchars. I have seen him, and he is dangerously ill.'

Helen grabbed at Margaret's arm.

'You must bring your medicines and save him! We have come too far that he should die. We know he is an innocent.'

Margaret closed her eyes as she replied.

'Helen, you will need to be very brave.'

Helen began to shout.

'No, he must not die – with God's help he will not! You have medicines and we know he had nothing to do with the robbery. He cannot die now!'

Margaret shook her head.

'My dear, listen. I have been with him most of the night. He is as well as we can expect, given his injuries. He has the medicine he needs.'

'Then I must go to him,' said Helen. 'Tell me where he is – he needs me.'

She reached out to Margaret, who replied softly.

'My dear girl, sometimes we cannot have what we would wish. Things are not meant to be, and we must accept … Julia Coatsworth is with John and, whether he lives or dies, he is hers. They love each other. I tried to tell you that true love requires two devoted people – two people who recognise something fundamental in each other. John Deuchars does not love you; he loves Julia Coatsworth.'

Helen pushed Margaret away roughly. Through tears she saw that a child was standing close by, silently watching them. He held all his worldly possessions in a bundle of cloth. Wiping the sleep out of his eyes, he walked over to her and held out his hand. Helen saw how thin he was; he had nothing to eat. She rummaged in her bag. He took the food she offered, arranged the bundle of rags around his shoulders and walked slowly away. How Helen envied him. She sank to the ground, sobbing.

'Julia Coatsworth! What is she doing here with my John? How dare she go to him? She already has everything, she cannot have him too.'

Margaret Alexander laid down her bag of medicines in the dust and held Helen tightly. They knelt quietly together as the sun brought more heat to Patna.

Daniel Jennings's interview with his daughter that morning was short. Helen was surprisingly quiet, which was just as well because his patience was virtually exhausted. The Coatsworth girl had succeeded in moving Deuchars to the Alexander woman's bungalow. There the criminal was watched over by Badshah Raj and his crew. The world had gone mad! He had no suspect and a wrecked factory, and the Chinese traders had gone.

Jennings met a very pale Helen in the garden of the bungalow. He told her that she could forget John Deuchars, describing in detail the touching scenes between the lovers which a father should have spared his daughter. He added that the boy was likely to die anyway and urged her to accompany him back to Calcutta. He made it clear that there were other opportunities open to her if she was sensible and wished to avoid returning home penniless.

'I will not help you, Helen, if you are not prepared to help yourself.'

Before leaving to meet with the remaining Chinese traders, Jennings advised Helen to consider her position carefully. He would return the following day, but would not wait if she was not ready to leave. Helen did not argue. She remembered her conversation with Julia on the night of the ball, and how she had spoken of John's frequent visits to the Coatsworth mansion. She was too late; Julia Coatsworth was a thief, and John was glad to be stolen. It was so painful. She knew she needed to leave. It would be impossible to remain under the same roof as the lovers; it was more than she could bear. Margaret had insisted on bringing them to the bungalow so that she could treat John. Helen had listened to her father apologise for John's imprisonment, making it sound as if had been misinformed. He had also said that John's mistreatment must have occurred when he was away in the surrounding countryside trying to track the stolen goods. It was a lie but, thought Helen, *all men are liars.*

Helen could hardly bear to contemplate travelling. She felt tired and ill, but what did it matter? – nothing mattered any more. If the only immediate way out of this place was with her father, then so be it. She could not even talk with Margaret, who was wholly occupied in the sickroom.

It is amazing, thought Daniel Jennings, *what a difference one day can make.* After a short meeting with Margaret Alexander, he had in his possession a small blood-stained notebook. The bitch would not give him the other books and he was not in a position to insist, but at least he had this. Any involvement he may or may not have had in arresting the wrong man would be lost when the scandal recorded between the covers of this tiny book was revealed.

Jennings sat in the office of the ruined godown and perused again the contents of the little brown book. It looked like nonsense at first glance, but he had reread each page of tiny scribbled notes and drawings, and saw what must be done.

Jennings set off later that same morning for Mowbray's house in the hills above Patna, where it was cooler. He was feeling cheerful; all was right with the world. John Deuchars was recovering, his daughter had seen sense, and if he could apprehend the real culprit quickly he would actually enhance own reputation. Given the information in the notebook, it should not be too difficult. It hardly mattered to the Company if John Deuchars lived or died, but there had to be retribution. The Company was an unforgiving master. That impossible Alexander woman had refused – even now, when he said he was convinced – to give him all the evidence. She was keeping it, she said, as surety. The nerve of the woman!

In any event, Deuchars was no longer relevant. If he were to live, Jennings could hardly be responsible for excesses committed in his absence. Should he die, the only person to miss him would be Julia Coatsworth. Helen had a real admirer, not some feckless boy. She had attracted a man who really wanted her, a man with power and wealth. Jennings had explained all this to his daughter, and tried to make her see sense as they rode out of Patna together. She protested, of course, but he knew she was listening. He had reminded her that security and wealth was all that mattered; love a pathetic, emotional distraction. During the long, hot journey he sought to distance himself from the imprisonment of John Deuchars. He described how chaotic things were after the robbery.

'How was I to know the boy was innocent? Everything pointed to him. I am no mind-reader.'

He had tried to explain to Helen that his job was not always pleasant, and that sometimes mistakes were made. Helen did not respond, so he decided to save his energy and excuses for Sir Josiah.

Jennings was pleased to have separated Helen from the Alexander woman. He reflected to himself that, as usual in his eventful life, calm is eventually restored and all things are possible. Jennings and Helen made good progress and reached the bungalow, where Mr Hugh Mowbray was much recovered. Jennings promised his daughter that she would find the interview amusing.

Mr Mowbray still required his cushions. He said that, due to the shock of recent events, he was quite the invalid, but he welcomed Jennings and Helen warmly.

'My dear sir,' Mowbray said to Jennings. 'Have you got your man, the young rogue? I would wager you have, for you are a sharp fellow. Tell me about how it was done; is the villain alive or dead?'

'Oh,' replied Jennings. 'He is very much alive, Mowbray, very much so, and in the arms of our Home Secretary's daughter. We have made several interesting discoveries while we have been investigating the whole affair. In fact I could not be less interested in John Deuchars as I now have in my possession ...' – he took the notebook from his pocket – '... these rather puzzling documents. But let us leave that for the moment. You will firstly want to know that we have located your former assistant, Mr James Jackson. Are you not astonished? As you know, he was reported deceased some time ago. Yet he recently reappeared, albeit very temporarily. They found him – that is to say, most of him. I understand the villains who left him to die first removed pieces of him. In fact they altered him horribly, by all accounts. He had a pretty poor time of it.'

Mowbray paled and pursed his lips, but rallied.

'Indeed, this is most odd,' he said. 'You say he is indeed dead – that is remarkable news. I need not write again to his mother. It would be most embarrassing to tell her he is alive when I had written to say with absolutely certainty that he was dead. Think of the poor woman's surprise! Now you say he has died again, in a manner of speaking. You must know that in my mind he has been dead all these months. I need not trouble a grieving mother a second time with more of the same, it would be too cruel. You say he suffered; this is most distressing.'

Mowbray walked slowly across the room; extracting his handkerchief, he moved it to his eyes.

'Tell me,' he said in tones of sadness, 'tell me how he died, the poor young man. Did you talk to him before he closed his eyes on this wicked world?'

Jennings did not immediately answer; he was much struck by Mowbray's composure.

'Before he died,' he presently replied, 'Mr Jackson was able to enlighten us as to the facts surrounding the recent robbery at the Patna factory. He reported other interesting detail about the criminal movement of goods.'

Mowbray stood completely still.

'My dear Jennings, how very interesting. Tell me more. Was he able to give you any evidence of the identity of the thieves? Perhaps a name, or a description of these miscreants? I have been here all this while, but I am as keen as you to find the culprits. I have been absent from the factory for some considerable time due to my health. As you know, the young villain John Deuchars was there each day with every opportunity for scheming and planning …'

'Oh,' interrupted Jennings. 'I don't think Deuchars had much to do with the robbery. I think there was a far more experienced hand at work. Someone, perhaps, who has worked for the Company for many years and who, feeling passed over by lesser men, was tempted. You know as well as I do, Mowbray, that too many demands on the purse can corrupt an honest man. Do you know of anyone who might be so corrupted?'

Mowbray stroked the shiny pearl buttons on his pale silver-and-mustard silk waistcoat.

'I have served the Company all my life,' he began again in a peeved tone. 'I had hoped for preferment before now, but circumstances …' He looked from Jennings to Helen and back, and continued, 'I do not feel, sir, that these things should be discussed in front of your daughter. I should not like my own girls to hear such tales.'

When Jennings did not ask Helen to withdraw, Mowbray continued.

'I say, what are you implying, sir? Say what you mean at once! I have nearly died in the service of this Company. I am a Company man these twenty years. I am a true and loyal servant and I hope you would not imply that I am somehow embroiled in this nasty …'

Mowbray stopped, noticing that Jennings held something. It was a small brown leather book – Mowbray's own book, compiled over the years with neatly drawn diagrams of the godowns and his calculations for the making, storage and transportation of opium.

His books contained careful details of the working arrangements within the factory, its very heartbeat. The 'Mowbray Method' had been spurned as too detailed for widespread Company use. His work had been unappreciated by fools who had never been inside a godown – men fresh out of school, who did not understand the complexities of the manufacture of opium and the management of its production. He still had the letter in which Sir Josiah had described his recording system as 'fussy'. That had been so hurtful, but he had continued to use the 'Mowbray Method'. He had so neatly and so carefully recorded all the workings of the factory; he recorded how much opium was produced, all wastage, amounts to be shipped. Such detail could not be challenged because no other person kept such beautiful records.

The books were his property, but now here was Jennings with one of them. The scoundrel was probably trying to steal his system. What could you expect? – they were letting anyone into Company business nowadays. The Company was full to the brim of second-rate aristocrats and useless boys, all halfwits. Hard work and devotion simply didn't matter anymore; practical men were no longer valued.

Jennings looked at Mowbray, who had attempted to snatch the book from his hand. Jennings fingered the pages as he spoke.

'I understand you might have expected more substantial rewards for your twenty-five years, which have not been forthcoming. I would sympathise with you if my disposition allowed it. Mowbray, you are beyond any assistance now. You have squandered countless opportunities down the years to make yourself rich. You belong to that generation of Company men who enjoyed the freedom and opportunity to bleed this country of every ruby it possessed. You could have had everything and gone home a nabob. It is so sad – here you remain in your old age, working in this heat for a pittance. A poor man still when others have gone home to their country estates long years ago.'

Jennings was enjoying himself, and continued, 'Why did you not make more of your time in India? You would not be standing here now, a common thief – a murderer, even. I cannot understand why you have not long since retired. You could be sitting on a fortune. If only you had been even slightly talented! Why, man, there were flags up and down the Hooghly these years past. Why were you not extorting for all you were worth? I tell you, I should have liked a free hand ten years ago. You could have gone home to a castle, and yet here you are, a common thief condemned by your own work.'

Jennings waved the small brown book in front of Mowbray.

'You idiot,' he went on, 'there are even notes as to how to transport the goods out of the area unseen, all here for the perusal of the court. A man must be much more inventive and careful to make money in the Company now. Things have changed, and you have had to make do with very slim pickings of late. I can understand the temptation – Coatsworth brought out here to run things, and you thought it was your turn. You told everyone it would be you next, then to be overlooked – and he is so much younger than you, with so much less experience. It is cruel, and I can understand that it would make any man bitter to have to serve the man who destroyed your dreams.'

Mowbray twisted in his shoes and pulled violently at the buttons of his waistcoat, so that two came off. He held them in his dimpled hands, rolling them back and forth like coins. They were large freshwater pearls and set off the silver-and-mustard silk beautifully. Mowbray was sweating profusely and as he wiped his brow the buttons slipped from his hands and fell to the floor. He made to grab them, but his wet, fat fingers could not catch them. Helen felt almost sorry for him as his face folded on its many creases and his shoulders heaved.

Mowbray suddenly lurched forward, moving quite swiftly for a man of his proportions. He snatched again at the book in Jennings's hand, succeeding in grabbing it, and held it to his chest. As he did so, he came close to Jennings's face so that even the bold Jennings stepped backwards.

Saliva ran down Mowbray's chin, and his voice was shrill as he spat out his words.

'I am owed as much as I have taken, and more. Men have gone home and bought titles and estates. I have not had justice; I have not had what was my due. In the old days I did not have to account for what I was able to secure for myself. Coatsworth always insisted on his cut because he was too lazy to shift for himself. It was the done thing to look after the Company first but also one's superior. I did not mind because there should have been enough for all in those days. We took what was our due, do you hear, and then we took more. The man before Coatsworth was greedy; he took everything and left me hardly enough. I have always been a loyal servant compared to some I could name. The Company looked the other way. All I needed was a little more time.'

Mowbray plucked at his waistcoat as if trying to remove the tangle of plants woven into the gorgeous satin.

'I have never been lucky,' he moaned. 'I have had reverses which were not of my making and there are always tribes of relatives at home.' He was plaintive now. 'I have worked my bones to dust in this heat. What have I taken? Almost nothing. Those Calcutta merchants lost everything in '15 and I had to start again. Since they stopped my small lines of enterprise and sent me home in '26, I have had such a drain on my funds. Jennings, you understand, I have my wife and girls at home to keep right. They are all of them ugly and none of them wed. We are reduced to stealing bales of poor-quality cotton to sell on the streets. Then there is my family here, my lovely Bibbi, and our boys. You know how it is, Jennings. How is a man to manage his affairs without some ingenuity, some small trade on the side? Would you have had me part with my beautiful Bibbi? Everyone knows that loneliness can kill a man here. I have been in daily expectation of death. Why should I not live well? I have seen so many good boys die, just fade away because of lack of preferment. I had no choice – a man without connections to Lord This or Lady That has to shift for himself. My income is now sadly decreased, and my situation will not improve after Sir Alfred's reforms. He will ruin us making this new India of his, giving preferment to natives. I ask you!'

He appealed to Jennings, and then to Helen.

'The problem with that last young man, Jackson, was unfortunate but he would ask questions and he was so quick. There is nothing quite as dangerous as an inquisitive young mind. He had to be silenced.'

Jennings noted that Mowbray had started to shake, but still he continued.

'I would not have wished Jackson dead. It gives me no pleasure to have to write to those poor mothers about their boys. In any event, the last one was not well, and would have died anyway. I encouraged him to take his medicine, but he overdid the poppy; he could not let it go. It was likely that India would have taken him as she takes others. You must understand, Jennings, he could not be taken back to Calcutta in his condition. I arranged that he should stay here in Patna and he organised that a small amount of goods might go astray now and then. It was never intended that an amount should be taken which would draw too much attention, especially as the Company had already noticed small discrepancies. He lost control; the smugglers were greedy and he was weak. When they asked me to come to manage things again I thought I could sort it all out. I realised quickly that things had progressed too far.'

Mowbray shook his head as he continued.

'He could not speak coherently when I last saw him, though he might have talked to others. They are ruthless, the opium traders, and they are off the leash now – you know they are. They have to be ruthless to get the opium past the Chinese authorities. I am not heartless; I do regret that he had to die, because he was a good boy. I have had so many good boys – some of them have done well, seen how things stood. Some of them have been helpful, but I have had to manage things with those who have not.'

It suddenly occurred to Jennings that Jackson might not be the first young Company man to die very young. Even Jennings was revolted by Mowbray, his pathetic weakness, his justification for murder. Those soft, flabby hands and beautiful waistcoats.

Mowbray was wild-eyed now; his hands worked together palm on palm and he shook his head vigorously as he spoke.

'John Deuchars was not a good boy. He was another who would leap past me for a choice posting. He was too clever by half – caught on fast, that one. He wormed his way into Sir Josiah's favour, always taking tea with him and lusting after the daughter. I wanted John Deuchars out of the way as soon as I could manage it. Why, if I had let him he could even have taken my position here, such as it is. I know they think me too old. Well, I will not be overlooked again – no, I will not.'

He now held a handful of pearl buttons, turning them over in his sticky hands. He moaned as they slipped out of his grasp.

'It's all such a mess, and I am ruined unless we can come to some agreement. If I caused trouble for you by sending you a note to get you away from the factory, you must understand why it had to be done. I could not have a man as sharp as you loitering around, but nobody will blame you, a man tireless in pursuit of his duty.'

He looked at Jennings and his voice became steadier.

'I have a tidy amount of money, which you could have were you to look the other way. We could all start again, a clean sheet. We can say there had been a mistake and that John Deuchars *is* the thief. Who would believe that mad old Scotswoman? The books can disappear; so could she and her evidence. The half-man she found, we would say he had been attacked by dacoits or set upon by animals – for who is to know, if we stick together? There is always a trader who will take goods directly from a Company man. I have more opium cakes stored away for a rainy day; you could have those, too. I have been every inch the loyal servant of the Company. I do not deserve ruination and disgrace.'

Mowbray sank to his knees weeping loudly, his hands groping the dusty floor in search of the lost pearl buttons.

'Yes,' said Jennings, hesitating to consider the offer while looking down at Mowbray as he grovelled on the floor. 'I suppose you may have more valuables stashed away and, to own the truth, your offer is tempting.' He turned to Helen. 'What do you think, my dear? Should we take his money?'

Helen had retreated to the dark long wall of the bungalow. She shuddered and turned her head away. Jennings smiled and faced Mowbray.

'My daughter thinks not. In any case, I have already seen beneath your floorboards and have liberated a tidy quantity of goods. You would be wise not to compound your thievery by alerting Sir Josiah to stolen goods under the floor, I think. I am in no doubt that my future needs would be best served by handing you over to Sir Josiah. You must be exposed if I am to advance my cause. I will make my name by uncovering your doings and putting all to rights. You are, as you have suggested, quite ruined. In fact, I think you will hang.' Jennings continued softly, 'I have sympathy for you, but you have been, how shall we say? ... careless. Come, man, get up from the floor − grovelling to me will not help you. Ask yourself, would a Company man howl like a baby?'

But, say what he would, Jennings could not make Mowbray stop.

It is a strange thing, the human spirit − it is the vital force which keeps us alive. As Mr Mowbray had predicted, India was, in the end, too much for him. It is fitting that he rests in Indian soil where Indian grubs can get at him. They will gorge on his flesh, as he fed on the very flesh of India.

On the whole, Mr Mowbray's family received the news of his death calmly. A cheque was sent home to his wife and daughters, as the Company did not want a scandal given the recent parliamentary scrutiny. The Company's will and bond branch wrestled with the last will and testament of Mr Hugh Mowbray for some considerable time. Early financial assistance from the Company was especially welcome to Mrs Mowbray and her girls. The family felt that the size of the cheque was fitting and proportionate to the regard in which Mr Mowbray had been held. They were not surprised that he had been taken, because Mr Hugh Mowbray had always been emphatic on leaving them, that India would be the death of him − and so it was.

Chapter Thirteen

It was weeks before the remaining party were ready to move from Patna. Daniel Jennings, having gone on ahead with Helen, had made good use of his time in Calcutta. He was able to inform Sir Josiah Coatsworth of recent events in Patna and describe the regrettable misunderstanding which had led to the imprisonment of John Deuchars. Jennings explained that this had been the fault of locals who had provided misleading information, and that he had perhaps been overzealous in the Company's interests. In this way he felt he had been able to present himself in the most favourable light possible. This was helped by his having Helen with him on two of his most difficult visits to Sir Josiah.

He also included in his narrative a particularly complimentary account of Miss Julia's heroic actions in saving John Deuchars from certain death. When Julia returned home her father was not as furious with her as she had thought he might be. In any event, by that stage he was altogether preoccupied with other important matters and did not wish to imprison his future son-in-law. Sir Josiah merely wished, as he had said many times before, that Julia had been shipped home to be refined into an English lady just like her mother. He acknowledged that it was entirely his fault that she had been used to running about like a wild creature. Sir Josiah declared himself truly shocked when he was told of the wickedness and disloyalty of Hugh Mowbray. He had the fellow down as a fool, but not a murderous one.

Sir Josiah thought long and hard about how he might explain the actions of a Company man to the Governor-General, and how to prevent the matter becoming public knowledge. He had wrestled with the dilemma as to whether Hugh Mowbray should be subject to the full weight of Company law or be quietly transferred somewhere malarial. In the event, his death made things much easier for the Home Secretary. He was able to keep the matter out of the Calcutta press by laying all blame for the robbery on the dacoits. He was aided in this because the last thing a new Governor-General wants is scandal.

In private, he shared his thoughts with close Company men.

'It is often the case,' said the poet in him, fingers carefully arranged together as if in prayer, 'that the sons of England come to the pagoda tree and shake its shining branches. Some are lucky enough to gather up the diamonds and rubies which fall from the boughs at their feet. Some are not so lucky; they are destined to die, and their bones lie whitened by the sun at the base of the said tree.' It was meant to have both pathos and humour. It went down so well that he repeated it often. The reaction of his audiences pleased him very much. Everyone agreed that it was a blessing that Mowbray had shown good sense enough to do the decent thing and die.

Margaret Alexander, who always advocated that deeds were more important than words, organised the making of a suspended travelling seat for John to minimise the jarring on the journey home. They planned to make their way slowly down the river. She would have preferred to keep him still for longer, but they had to leave soon to avoid travelling in the hottest months. John was still very weak. Helen had not explained to Margaret that she had to leave, but when they saw each other again in Calcutta she told her that the storm had passed. She would not indulge in self-pity. Helen admitted publicly that she had been foolish to allow herself to feel so much for a man she hardly knew, but she did not believe it in her heart. She had learned from her experience and was glad that John Deuchars had lived. She told Sir Josiah that she wished to put the whole affair behind her, which he received as welcome encouragement. She had seen Julia Coatsworth and had told her she was glad to have been the instrument of aiding her cousin. Julia had declared her to have been very brave, but she did not think Julia was taken in at all.

Helen recalled that she had promised never to allow herself to be placed in a position of weakness. Now she repeated this as a solemn vow to herself and felt something shift in her soul. She had visited John only once since their return to Calcutta. Although he was astonished to see her, she did not tire him with explanations. What would be the point? He was not yet strong, and this was not the time or place. Perhaps one day she would tell him, but not now.

On a very hot day in July, Margaret sat in the dark recesses of her veranda, talking quietly with Helen. Speaking softly and comfortingly, she had offered her a home. She even ventured that she might join her in her mission permanently. Would that not provide a sense of purpose, the contemplation of a life of service to others? It would justify her long journey. Was that not preferable to living in her father's house? Helen loved Margaret dearly, but did not think that such a life of privation would suit her. She said she appreciated Margaret's efforts to help, but had made her decision. She did not look directly at Margaret when she said, 'I will secure the rewards I long ago promised myself when mother and I were so uncomfortable. I find I am no longer an idealist. You must not worry about me – I know what I am doing.'

Helen had not come all the way to India for nothing. She would have given everything to be with John, but that was the past. They speak of a bride price; she had remembered hers now, and it was very high. She was no speculator; she wanted certainty. She would set out her own terms, and they would be hard to meet.

'I had thought I could help John Deuchars in his life's work,' she said to Margaret. 'I thought I could be something to him and that together we could build a life, but I do not think Sir Josiah is an entirely finished piece of work, so we shall see.'

'To attach yourself without love, to calculate in this way …' said Margaret, frowning.

Helen was silent, and Margaret shook her head; there was nothing more to say.

In due course Daniel Jennings returned to Patna with his two British officers and sepoys from the 33rd Regiment. He made a great show of interrogating the whole of the Patna district, in the certain knowledge that chasing the 'dacoit robbers' was akin to seeking out the *rakas*. It did, however, provide a good opportunity to discuss arrangements for shipment and management of the following year's harvest. Growers were already predicting a plentiful and unspoiled crop due to the auspicious westerly winds. The contents of Mowbray's bungalow and satisfactory discussions with Sir Josiah resulted in his being able to settle all his debts in Calcutta and reassured him that family fortunes were mending.

He had, it is true, endured a rather awkward conversation with Sir Josiah, who reminded him he was not above Company law himself and that he needed to keep the savagery of his men in check. At first John Deuchars was determined to press charges of some kind, although Jennings had sent his profuse apologies for what he called 'an unfortunate misunderstanding'. Deuchars insisted that amends be made to Amil and his family, and this had cost him dear. It was worth the money, as the matter was then dropped.

Daniel Jennings did not think that in the future he would ever need to worry about money. Sir Josiah was an understanding man, who knew that gentlemanly principles did not always apply in the field. Jennings was also reminded by his daughter that he had not yet sent assistance to her mother. He had assured her that, in the fullness of time, he would certainly do so. Privately, he thought that it might have to be the following year, given the extension he was planning to his new home off Old Court House Street. In any case, Helen would be sure to do something for her mother herself should she become someone of consequence. He would not press her on that score, just in case he upset certain matters which were progressing very nicely.

On a bright morning in February 1831, Lady Coatsworth left off the preparations for her departure from Calcutta. She looked down from the balcony of her magnificent house on the banks of the Hooghly River, from which she had an unrivalled view of the bay.

'Well, go, then,' she murmured. 'Go back to England; I have not finished with India quite yet.'

Her fingers played with the most enormous string of large creamy pearls which wound around her neck and over her bosom. She carefully smoothed her luxurious indigo silk gown, while the maidservant adjusted the coverlet on her bed.

It was just after dawn and the heat was starting to seep into the day. As shafts of sunlight fell into the room, the large diamond on her left hand caught the bright morning sunshine in its very centre. It seemed to send a stream of light out into the bay. Helen stood and watched the fleet of East Indiamen as small colourful specks crowded against the ships' rails. She strained her eyes but could not make them out. Helen did not know it, but John and Julia Deuchars were already below deck on the *Cornwallis*, making sure of their accommodation. She could not see them and yet she was certain that they were standing on the rail looking out to sea and towards their new life at home in England.

The ships hardly seemed to move at first. They hung suspended in the heat haze, and then, one by one, followed each other out of the harbour, plunging over the bar on a glistening pathway of sunlight that stretched to the horizon. Helen stood and watched them until their sails were only just visible.

She shaded her eyes as she murmured:

'Look out into the streaming sun, that shining ribbon of sea,

Say farewell on a clear day, to one who was dear to me.

Now just a shimmer on top of the waves, part of the thundering roar,

I loved you once, I love you still, but you are mine no more.'

Helen smiled, turned and moved slowly back into the room. Her maid waited only a moment before silently following her inside and closing the shutters. Helen blinked, adjusting her eyes to the half-light. As she did so, the image of a small ship sailing away on a bright blue sea appeared before her. It seemed to dance on the shimmering waves. She thought for a moment that she might just reach out and touch it. Without thinking, Helen stretched her hand out into the darkness of the room. Then she started as Sir Josiah pulled her fingers roughly to his mouth and kissed them.

Epilogue

Mrs Margaret Alexander was soon afterwards provided with new whitewashed premises and significant resources to continue her work. A small plaque on the wall outside confirmed that the new buildings were provided by her friend and loyal supporter in India, Lady Josiah Coatsworth. It was reported by the Calcutta press that this lady had recently accompanied her husband to his new posting at Bangalore, and is said to be expecting her first child.

Glossary

aba	Loose-fitting overgarment
ayah	Native-born nurse or maidservant
batta	Special allowance made to officers, soldiers, or other public servants in the field
chirata	Bitter herb, used in the management of fevers and upset stomach, loss of appetite and other digestive complaints; known as the 'Indian gentian'.
chittak	Unit of weight in India; 1/16th of a seer
churrundar	Cabin boy
dacoit	Member of a class of robbers in India and Burma, who plunder in armed bands
dolai	Stuffed quilt to keep travellers warm
gatta	Sweetmeat made of molasses
ghur	Hole in the ground filled with straw and lit in the evening to provide heat
godown	Warehouse
Mahratta	Elite member of a group of castes, largely made up of a rural class of peasant cultivators, landowners and soldiers; famed in history as yeoman warriors and champions of Hinduism. Now usually spelled 'Maratha'.

palanquin	Covered conveyance, usually for one person, consisting of a large box carried on two horizontal poles by four or six (rarely two) bearers
punkah	Large, swinging fan fixed to the ceiling and pulled by a servant (punkah wallah)
raka	Evil spirit or will-o'-the-wisp that tries to mislead travellers
seer	Unit of weight in India; approximately one kilogram
sitalpati	A kind of mat which feels cold by nature, made from cane or murta plants
suttee	Funeral custom in which a widow immolates herself on her husband's pyre or takes her own life in another fashion shortly after her husband's death (banned in Bengal from 1829)
thagi	Cutthroat or ruffian (also "Thug", a member of a group of criminals)
thuggee	System of robbery and murder practised by the Thugs
zamindar	Aristocratic title. Typically hereditary, zamindars held enormous tracts of land and control over their peasants, from whom they reserved the right to collect tax on behalf of imperial courts or for military purposes.

www.ingramcontent.com/pod-product-compliance
Lightning Source LLC
Chambersburg PA
CBHW051509170626
46811CB00002B/720